SCE[N]
OF
OBSESSION

SHANEN RICCI

Scent of Obsession
Copyright © 2021 Shanen Ricci

All rights reserved. Without limiting the rights under copyright reserved above, no part of this publication may be reproduced, stored in or introduced into retrieval system, or transmitted, in any form, or by any means (electronic, mechanical, photocopying, recording, or otherwise) without the prior written permission of both the copyright owner and the above publisher of this book.

This is a work of fiction. Names, characters, places, brands, media, and incidents are either the products of the author's imagination or are used fictitiously. The author acknowledges the trademarked status and trademark owners of various products referenced in this work of fiction, which have been used without permission. The publication/use of these trademarks is not authorized, associated with, or sponsored by the trademark owners.

Cover designer: Maria Spada
Editor: One Love Editing
Proofreader: All Encompassing Books
Formatter: Stacey Blake

Playlist

"Devil Devil" MILCK

"Gods and Monsters" Lana Del Rey

"Me And The Devil" Soap&Skin

"Les Yeux Noirs" Pomplamoose

"Libella Swing" Parov Stelar

"Master Mirror" Ashley Serena

"Everybody wants to rule the world" LORDE

"Underworld" CYPRSS

"Persephone" Tamino

"Black Magic Woman" VCTRYS

"Fire meets fate" Ruelle

"Intertwined" Satin Puppets

"Monster" MILCK

"Become the beast" Karliene

"Other Side" Ruelle

"Carol of the bells" Tommee Profitt

Prologue

Beware of the Witch.

Removing petals at first bloom,

She's gifted with a curse.

Floral, oriental, woody, fresh scents have no secrets for her.

Beware of the Witch.

She'll put a spell on you.

Sweet and innocent, but yet poisonous.

A dark secret she's hiding.

Beware of the Witch.

Because to every Witch, there is a Devil.

Chapter 1

Radcliff

"You're disappointing me, Eugene."

I rolled my signature tarot card between my fingers, eying the impostor's disappearing smile. His heart leaped into his throat. Dread twisted in his gut. He adopted a submissive posture, curving his back and bending his shoulders forward.

"Please, Mr. Radcliff, what you're asking me is impossible. I've tried and—"

The thundering sound of my hand against my desk echoed across the stygian manor, muting him with terror. His face was ashen when, by mistake, he met my hellish stare and caught a glimpse of my monstrous face in the midst of the shadows. He bowed his head, his chin trembling.

"You failed whilst taking the generous amount of money I

offered you for a job you assured me you were capable of doing. In addition to lying and not fulfilling your contract, you tried to fool me." My physical appearance was enough to make him shrink back in horror, but my apparent calm was a deadly weapon. I didn't have to threaten him; he knew he had no other choice if he didn't want to lose everything.

"I can't pay you back yet. I—I don't have any money, but I—" *Tik. Tak.* His eyes darted from left to right as he struggled to conceal his panic. "I have a niece! Her name's Lily Bellerose," he shrieked, his voice on edge.

"Bullshit, Eugene. It all comes down to you being a fool without a poker face." I cracked my knuckles, tired of this nonsense.

This pathetic fool had lost my money to gambling debts and spending more than he could on materialistic objects and women. He wore a pitiful designer watch, trying to belong to a social status that was out of reach for him. A crook—and not even a good one.

The point was, I couldn't care less about some random girl, and I was even less interested in sequestering anyone. That's what I got for doing business with *The Fool*.

"She—She's one of the greatest noses. I've never seen anything like it." *Now that's interesting.* "She inherited the talent of my sister. Believe me—" *Surely not.* "I may be an impostor, but she isn't. I'll get her to come to you—you'll see it in front of your own eyes."

"And why would I waste my time with her."

"Because I can convince you. I have a secret… Something I've never told anyone. Something big."

LILY

The flower shop owner elegantly wrapped and tied my bouquet with an ivory ribbon.

The scent of the Christmas's Tale bouquet filled my lungs. The cherry-red roses bloomed my heart, along with the sweet scent of the white amaryllis, also known as the Christmas lily, one of my mother's favorite flowers. In fact, she loved lilies so much—her favorite being the lily of the valley—that she named me after them.

Pure, plain, and perfect Lily.

"That'll be twenty-four euros, mademoiselle."

I snapped back from my thoughts when the vendor handed me my bouquet that I held inside my arms like a mother with her precious baby. I searched for my last remaining euros inside my floral-print wallet, blaming myself for the guilty pleasure I'd stumbled upon. The coins fell on the desk, and I counted each coin separately, the judging gazes of the people around us hastening me to hurry.

"Here, let me get this." Adonis handed his premium credit card to the vendor with a dazzling smirk.

"No, Adonis! You don't have to—" I defended pointlessly.

"It'll be my Christmas gift to you, princess."

He wrapped an arm around my shoulder, and I compressed the bouquet tighter to my chest. I wasn't used to being called princess. I'd grown up on the bad side of the fairy tale. I was either the fair maiden without a story worth telling or the witch. It was a nickname given to me during my youth, because of my addiction to scents and flowers. A nickname that brought me anything but pain.

"Thank you," I said in a low voice out of shyness before my gaze drifted to the store owner, who couldn't keep her eyes from Adonis. "Merry Christmas."

"Merry Christmas," she responded to Adonis, captivated by his charm.

After all, Adonis was, just like his name, unfairly gorgeous with his ocean eyes and golden hair. He smelled of purple—raspberry, lavender, and heliotrope—the kind of scent that everyone likes, but it wasn't earth-shattering to me.

Once he'd collected his card, we strolled toward the exit, me inhaling the scents of the bouquet, him making everyone succumb with a devastating smile, the doorbell chiming when we stepped out.

Adonis was my only friend in Paris. We'd met in a garden in Saint-Germain-des-Prés and immediately grew our friendship based on our mutual passion for perfume, even if I was on the creative side and he on the luxury one—born on a land of milk and honey.

His father, Christian Carmin, was the CEO of Carmin, the giant of the most prestigious luxury cosmetic group, and Adonis was the only heir. He was destined to have the world bow at his feet while I was the outsider.

Or, most likely, an abnormal twenty-one-year-old woman who'd grown up with the belief she had a guardian angel watching over her. And if that wasn't enough, I saw the world through different eyes (or, in my case, my nose). Probably a gift—or a curse—I inherited from my mother. I was convinced she would have become one of the greatest noses of all time if she had been still of this world.

But life was not a bed of roses.

Adonis and I ambled through the small-pebbled roads and cobbled lanes filled with cafés and eateries in the direction of my apartment. Trailing ivy covered the houses, along with winter decorations. Cars couldn't venture through the narrow lanes, giving us a semblance of nature and poetry.

"So, I'm off to a family dinner for Christmas with my dad, and then we're flying to Italy until New Year's Eve." Adonis's attention was on his phone, texting abundantly.

"That's great you'll be able to spend more time together."

"Right." He snorted. "He's just missing his yacht. Sometimes he cares more about it than his own son. Anyway, do you have any plans with your uncle?"

"Of course." I beamed.

Uncle promised we would eat a Christmas dinner together for once. My uncle wasn't perfect, but he was my only family left. My father hadn't acknowledged my existence since the day I was born, and I never knew any of my grandparents.

"That's cool." He stopped in front of my building, putting away his phone, which kept on vibrating inside the pocket of his suit trousers. "I guess my dad is getting impatient. Anyway, there is something I wanted to tell you."

I raised an eyebrow, waiting for him to continue.

"New Year's, you and I, we're going to a masquerade ball." My lips parted, and before I could ask anything else, he added, "Not negotiable. I'll pick you up."

Recreating a formula was an easy task for me. But I'd tried countless times to create a revolutionary perfume, and it always ended up soulless and uninspired. Mom used to say I needed to create a masterpiece. She was right—the world would never be handed to me on a silver platter. If I wanted an empire, I would have to give my whole soul for it.

Truth was, I wasn't satisfied with any fragrances I created. I erased them. Trashed them. Broke them. I gave all of myself to my creations, drowning my loneliness in them. Scents had shaped my reality—they were my life—and I was laying the foundation of a boring average.

I tucked the fruity fragrance I'd reproduced from my uncle's favorite perfume inside a wrapping paper, then added a ribbon to my gift when I heard the angry honking of cars on the street filtering in, the wall of my slums cracking, and the old landlady of the building complaining to my neighbors. Madame Laval. *Crap.*

She was probably grumbling about the way I cleaned the bathrooms. They had to be cleaned often, since none of the rooms on the upper floors, including mine, had toilets included in their chambers.

I rushed to find the keys to my apartment, grabbed my vest, and headed downstairs in a hurry. I'd made a deal with Madame Laval three years ago: I would clean the entire old building in exchange for the *chambre de bonne* on the roof. This opportunity had given me time to study and to focus on my perfumes.

Plus, my uncle lived just downstairs. It wasn't that bad. From my window and the ramp of the roof on my balcony, I could peer at the Eiffel Tower when the sky was clear. I'd made a promise to myself years ago that one day, I'd have the world.

I bolted down the wooden staircase carpeted in a vibrant red. Thankfully, Madame Laval was inside the tiny elevator, which was squeezed in the middle of the stairs. I successfully avoided being seen through the metal cages by hiding behind the railing.

Finally reaching my uncle's apartment, I uncovered the key from under the doormat and unlocked the door. "Hi, Uncle! It's Lily."

He didn't reply. I wandered across the apartment searching for him, wrinkling my nose. It smelled terrible. Probably from the dirty clothes on the floor and the flies near the trash. *Uncle Eugene, you're a mess.*

I sauntered past a note on the fridge.

I left you a piece of Christmas log. I'll probably be late, don't wait up.
Merry Christmas, my Lily!

Not again. He promised. I didn't think twice before calling him.

I waited for him to pick up, my fingers rubbing against each other. One beep. Yet another. I tapped my foot on the floor.

The beeps stopped. I hastened to speak. "Hi, Uncle, where are you?"

"I'm sorry, my car broke down halfway between Normandy and Paris. I won't be able to be here tonight," he excused himself. He didn't seem to be by a highway. There was a din in the background that sounded like laughing children.

Frowning dubiously, I ignored the gut feeling twisting my stomach. "Oh, I'm sorry to hear that. Can I do anything?"

"Did you get my gift?"

Gift? My gaze flicked over to a wrapped gift on the table. "Oh wait, let me see what it is!" I put my uncle on speaker mode, sat on the chair, and tore up the paper eagerly.

Excellence. The last Carmin perfume.

I swallowed my disappointment.

In the face of my silence, my uncle spoke again, his voice laced with worry. "You don't like it?"

Honestly? It smelled like cat piss with an average formula. There was nothing creative about it and no storytelling.

"Sure," I lied to not hurt his feelings.

My uncle wasn't rich, working as a chemistry teacher at the Paris Institute of Perfume. Before that, he was a renowned nose at one of the biggest perfume brands in France. He wasn't crawling under debt, but I knew he was struggling financially. He'd already asked for my help a couple of times.

"But you shouldn't have spent that amount of money on it." A hundred and twenty euros for *this* was outrageous.

"But you love that perfume, no?"

Uncle Eugene, you've lost your touch.

"It's the No. 27 of Carmin that I love," I chuckled. The 27 was Carmin's best-selling perfume. Released years ago, it remained a masterpiece. I had asked Adonis about it, but the noses were their company's best-kept secret.

"Right, I—"

"Eugene, the dinner is getting cold," a woman whispered to him through the phone.

Wait, had he lied to me? My heart thumped wildly at the thought. My gaze stopped in the void as I denied all the emotions begging to consume me.

"Well, Lily, I've got to go… Merry Christmas, darling."

I faked a smile, keeping the pitch of my voice calm, not wanting him to be concerned about me. "To you too, Uncle."

I hung up.

I took the rest of the log out of the freezer and grabbed a spoon mechanically. The carnival of laughter from the neighbors filled the void of the apartment, and I imagined the amber scent of tree sap, the vanilla-scented candles. The smell of their roast goose and turkey wafted up my nostrils.

A spoonful of the log iced my interior, driving me further away from the warmth of Christmastime. A peek at the happy posts on social media drove me closer to the realization I was once again alone.

At least on New Year's Eve I wouldn't be.

I had something to look forward to.

Chapter 2

Lily

6 days later

"Ravencliff Manor, home of the wicked and the sinners," exclaimed Adonis theatrically while driving along a narrow path under the moonlight.

"I can't believe we're actually going there," I muttered, the mist of my breath taking the shape of my hand against the car window.

Everyone was fascinated with Ravencliff Manor, a two-hour drive from Paris, to the point many tales were told. The most haunting one was from a woman who'd ended her life at the cliff. People said she became a somber spirit, inviting other lost souls to end their suffering. They would be endlessly condemned to spin inside the cursed ocean until the end of time. The other tales were either dark legends to scare children or a wicked fantasy to animate the nights of the pleasure-seeking elite.

As we sank into the hostile forest, the lifeless trees seemed to shut in, choking out the gleam of the moonlight to let the fog roll around like a breath. The howling of the wind and the thunder of the crashing waves on the hard rocks down the cliff was a sinister symphony to accompany inky black nightmares. The briny air of the ocean filled my nostrils; it smelled of storm and loneliness.

Even the car's heating couldn't warm us from the view of the manor. From afar, it looked like the perfect depiction of a desolate house. A fortress of evil whose somber edges were as thin as blades attempting to bleed the sky. Overhanging the hill, it blocked any light from entering, hiding in the shadow matching the murkiness of its occupant.

"How is he?" By "he," I was referring to *he who shall not be named*—Radcliff, the owner of the manor, the host, and the biggest mystery of tonight's New Year's Masquerade Ball. Like everyone in France, I'd heard of him and his uncanny reputation, but like most everyone else, I'd never encountered him.

My uncle had come to the manor a couple of times. He'd never brought me, though I guessed he had met Radcliff—not that we ever discussed him. No sane person would want to be involved with him anyway.

"He goes by the name Devil. He gives his signature card to people he does business with," Adonis replied while handing me his exclusive invitation. "The legend says that he can read your soul."

A tarot card.

Number XV.

The Devil.

My gaze slithered closely to the card, my fingers lingering on the drawing. A bad feeling crept through my spine. A grotesque beast with horns was seated on a throne, unyielding, a pentacle above his head. His chained slaves were holding grapes and a fire torch. They were completely at his mercy.

My curiosity couldn't be shut down, even though the message was clear—it was an upscale invitation to hell that people were willingly eager to savor.

"But if you ask me, he's more of a phantom," Adonis added with an angelic smirk that drew my attention to his dreamy dimples.

"How did you get that card?"

"It was my father's. Some dude working for the phantom came to our house and delivered it to me in person, since my father was absent. Dad doesn't even know I've stolen his invite to bring the prettiest girl in Paris with me for a night she'll never forget, but I'm sure he'd approve," he joked.

"You'll get into trouble for it." I chuckled. "But thank you." Tonight was my first event of this magnitude—or at all—and I was ready to step out of my comfort zone. I had never traveled anywhere or lived anything exciting.

After crossing the imposing gothic fence, where two gargoyle statues held guard, we escaped the rest of the hostile forest and arrived in front of the ghostly manor. "What—What's all this?" My eyes opened wide. People cosplaying sorcerers were rocking the night with African drum beats. The guests were dressed as eccentric Renaissance royalty, giggling and already drunk.

It was extreme.

Magnificent.

The reincarnation of one of the scandalous Great Gatsby parties at Dracula's manor on a dusky night.

"That is the Devil's work." Adonis raked a hand through his sleek hair and adjusted his royal blue costume in the mirror of the car. "Great parties, monstrous man. At least with a masquerade ball, he can hide how hideous he looks."

A jack with a pink wig and a parrot on his shoulder opened the car's door for us. Adonis handed him the keys to park it while my nose got drunk with the diverse scents coloring the night. It was an exotic firework, a watercolor painting of emotions colliding together.

"Hideous?"

Adonis didn't pay attention to my question, focused on tying his masquerade mask and completing his outfit with a golden feather hat. He was the epitome of Prince Charming—compared to me, who looked like I was in my undergarments. With a linen corset tightening my waist and pushing my breasts upward, my pristine white Grecian dress braced the curves of my hips perfectly—and because I was that obvious, I used lilies as jewels and hairpins.

"Why hideous?" I asked once more when he offered me his arm to stroll toward the entrance.

"Have you ever wondered why no one has ever truly seen his face? Why is he always hiding like a creature from a fable inside his gothic manor?"

I shook my head. I was so obsessed, living in my own universe, that I wasn't one to encourage nor entertain gossip for the simple reason that I, too, had been the main subject of it in the past. It was only a partiality of reality. An interpretation of one's soul.

"Well." Adonis whirled in front of me with a sly smirk. "Even your uncle admitted he had never seen *anything* like that."

"He's a person, Adonis, not a *thing*."

"You'd think that. He's a monster." Something dark slithered through my veins hearing Adonis's harsh words. I wondered if he wanted to scare me on purpose. "Don't worry, princess. I'd slay the beast for you if I had to. After all, I promised your uncle I'd keep an eye on you tonight." Of course, my uncle knew where Adonis was bringing me before I did.

"Your phones," the imposing security guard interrupted us at the gate, his glance flicking over a velvet box behind him.

We had no choice but to capitulate, giving our phones away for the rest of the night.

Adonis leaned toward me, whispering in my ear, "And of course he'd ask for complete privacy so no one can immortalize in pictures how repugnant he is."

He cracked a smile before using his natural charm to prove we were legitimate invited guests to this party. I gazed at the universe of sins around me. It was a perverted jungle in which the crowd surrendered to their obscure desires the moment they signed their names at the entrance.

I was an outsider at the gates of hell.

I tilted my head up to watch the stars sparkling through the dusky night and met the stare of a man with a grim figure. We were both static, as opposed to the extravaganza around us. Alone on the highest balcony, he reeked of superiority in a black satin costume without a single speck of color about him anywhere. Austere. Unwelcoming. I observed this man melting with the shadows, a cold shiver not leaving my back.

I was too far away to distinguish his gaze under his dark-silver Venetian mask, but I had no doubt his eyes were firmly set on mine. Each fiber of my body screamed at me with a deep intensity, *Turn away. That man is up to no good.* But being hidden behind my ivory-white mask gave me enough confidence to ignore my gut.

Just when I thought the man was carved in stone, he gave a slight nod in my direction. Was he greeting me? I swiveled my eyes in the opposite direction, feeling unveiled by him.

"Take this." The security guard handed me a jet-black ribbon, commanding me through gestures to tie it around my wrist. "Keep it," he ordered then, holding my stare as if he knew something I didn't.

I searched for Adonis's sign to enlighten me on the situation, but he seemed as clueless as me. Instead, he executed the guard's order, helping me to tie the ribbon on my wrist.

"Let's go," he said, sliding his hand behind my lower back, guiding us eagerly to the heart of the party.

On our way, my curiosity sparkled through my core, and I couldn't help but glance one last time at the balcony.

He was gone like an imaginary ghost.

"This is what I call a party," Adonis cheered, lifting his champagne glass and caviar toast.

The interior of the manor was pure madness. The ancient, warped staircases were filled with women acting like courtesans and men chasing after them. The old crystal chandeliers, covered in dust, were ignored by the show of the exuberant food. The whole place entailed debauchery in a sumptuous cacophony.

"Gentlemen, may I present you my beautiful escort for the night, Lily Bellerose."

The group of older men didn't bother to acknowledge me politely but instead took sight of my whole body, as if I were a pretty object on display.

"Exquisite," one commented.

I acted with a gracious smile like his comment didn't get to me. I'd developed the skill to bury my darkest emotions inside my head, creating my own Pandora's box. It was either self-preservation or because I chose to focus on the good. The hopeful.

A couple of laughs later and I had served my purpose for Adonis to win them over. I assumed they were business partners of his dad, since Adonis wished to be more involved in his father's business. When the group of men finally stepped away to start their night of depravity, Adonis's fingers brushed over my hand.

"I'll be back, okay?" he assured me.

I beamed, because that was the only choice. I couldn't beg him to stay with me. With a seductive wink, he rejoined the men, leaving me on my own.

My eyes, like magnets, darted instinctively to what or, more likely, who was standing at the dim edges of the room near the Grecian arch.

Him.

Confronted face-to-face with the grim spirit of earlier, he stood like a tenebrous mystery, hands in his pockets in the midst of the chaos. My lips parted in a daze. We observed each other from afar like two savage animals judging the unknown territory.

He was imposing and terrifying, not only from his impressive height but from the darkness that was emanating from him. His presence was larger than the room and would intimidate anyone. Sinister, with an impenetrable expression, it was impossible to imagine what this man was hiding.

I peeked at his strained muscles hidden underneath his suit, sensing the strength he was capable of when he made a card slide between his fingers mechanically, with scary ease.

A scandalous party thrown by a ghost.

A hideous man delivering pleasures.

A tale graved in a gloomy mystery.

A drunk woman collided with me while dancing ungracefully, spilling her drink on my white—now transparent—dress. I should have been embarrassed or pissed, but my first reflex was to look one more time at the arch. The haunting man was gone again, as if he were a product of my imagination.

I started pulling back the pieces of the puzzle together.

The man that everyone talks about but doesn't see.

The phantom.

A mystery.

I closed my eyes, replaying our encounter in my brain. I materialized the card rolling between his fingers. I zoomed in on the image. I was close. Just a little closer. I peeled my eyes open when the image surfaced in my mind, and I let out a sharp gasp at the realization of the truth.

Number XV.

The Devil.

By a twisted turn of fate, I had played a game of cat and mouse with the man known as the Devil.

Radcliff.

My heart palpitating from the rush of contradictory feelings I was experiencing, I had trouble breathing in this tight corset. I stormed across the room, looking for Adonis, but I was unable to find him.

I spun, seeing only the hard stares of the men through their masks, their laughter echoing inside the room. It was like I had jumped in water infested with sharks wanting my blood. I decided to retract from the main party, feeling uneasy.

My gut led me to a French garden, where long avenues of trees formed a mysterious path. Luckily for me, the courtyard was illuminated by sparkling lights. I could stay here for a moment. Finally able to take a deep breath, I let the fresh cold air caress my skin while the noise of the fountains leaped above the exuberance of the party, slowing my heart.

I let the moment take me away until I smelled something raw and powerful. A dark essence I'd never encountered before. Intrigued and magnetically attracted, I traipsed without thinking deeper onto the path.

I was possessed.

Bewitched.

That smell wasn't attractive nor welcoming. It could even be called repulsive, like a heavy patchouli that had turned wrong or a musty, cold basement smell. But it didn't stop me, because it had to hide something else. Jasmine was an intense and sensual scent, yet it could smell like dirty sex too, even sometimes bad—like pee because of the indoles. But no one would know since popular perfumers had stripped away all the skanky notes.

I stopped on my path when the lights leading to the greenhouse faded. I needed to gather my courage to solve the second mystery of the night. The greenhouse was illuminated—I could still make it. I rushed as fast as I could to it and unlocked the door. Once inside, I discovered the flower responsible for intoxicating my senses.

A corpse flower.

She was unique, overpowering all the flowers around her. Significantly taller than the others, and even taller than most humans, she had a spadix making her look like a giant calla lily. The top of the flower was different, more similar to a carnivorous plant—the one that would shut close and trap intruders. Thorns grew around the trap like teeth wanting to tear at you. She had several layers of petals, from a deep crimson purple with a touch of burgundy red. Protected and caged between the brambles and thorns, they encircled her stem, rising like a maleficent wall. At her roots, she grew petals the size of an ogre foot, where stems of small flowers bloomed next to it.

She belonged to a twisted fairy tale where the forever happy ever after had been rewritten by villains.

The lily of the valley was a symbol of purity. That monstrous flower was the opposite. It screamed of sins. I had found my extreme, something that could revolutionize the most boring of formulas.

A sweet scent which craved a dark, earthly one.

Light and darkness colliding to form the perfect essence.

A match made in heaven—or in hell.

She contained life and death within her, holding the power to immortalize a scent in time.

Inching toward the hostile flower, I reached out to steal a petal. Tonight, I had discovered my sin. I would become a thief.

Despite the repellent odor, underneath was a hidden scent that had the power to shatter all my nerves to the abyss of my soul. It was a common fact that sensory experiences triggered memories into the human soul; they were linked to our emotions.

In my case, I was visualizing me and my mother picking flowers in the countryside. I quivered, the smell transporting me into paradise. *A kiss that felt like a first. Lust. A glowing moon.* My heartbeat galloped. *Dark sheets smelling of patchouli.* My throat dried, the hair on my skin hissed. *A thunderstorm roaring, the black veil curtains swaying until—*

"What are you doing," a menacing voice resonated behind me. It certainly wasn't a question but a threat to face the consequences of my actions.

Pulling away from the corpse flower, I faced the imposing shadow. I hid the feeling of shame burning my core, a deathly stillness falling over me. The man took one careful step toward me, stepping into the light so I could see who he was.

Through his mask, I had a glimpse of his obsidian eyes, black with some unfathomable emotion. A few rebellious strands of his raven hair fell onto his forehead. He was merciless and undeniably dangerous, like a man who carried the scars of his past.

The tip of his cigar went red before he stubbed it out under his shoe, and he exhaled his smoke, which danced wickedly around me. I tried not to cough but failed when the leather taste of the smoke entered my mouth. My gaze drifted to the floor, and my eyes stung. When the smoke passed, only the stranger's dark essence of sandalwood remained.

I dared to lift my eyes up.

Radcliff.

My breaths turned shallow. Nervousness skittered across my core; my whole body petrified under his marbled stare that crept under my skin.

Run.

That's what any other person would have done. But I couldn't. My legs were glued to the floor. The presence of him transformed me into stone.

"Get out," his raspy voice ordered.

Monstrous…

Hideous…

The voice of Adonis echoed through my brain. Which monster was hiding behind the mask? Which dark secrets was this place covering?

It would be a lie to say I wasn't terrified.

But most importantly, I was dangerously obsessed.

"No," I defied him with a quivering voice.

Approaching midnight, fairy-tale princesses ran home to let the monsters own the night.

But I was no princess, after all.

I was the Witch.

Chapter 3

Radcliff

N o.

I inspired awe and terror in everybody. I was the one they called Monster behind my back but bowed to in front. Humans were cowards. I wouldn't complain—I gladly took advantage of their sins, building an empire on their weaknesses.

No was a word a wise person would never dare to speak to me. And yet, that woman stood there with a confidence and determination I'd never met in any being. She knew who I was. Her body language betrayed her—fists locked, body shaking, breaths shaky and short to the point she was suffocating in her corset.

Prey.

From the moment I laid eyes upon her, I concluded she had nothing to do with my world. That ridiculous white floral dress screamed of innocence in a place where people crave purity to corrupt. Needless to say, she was in her early twenties, ignorant, and clearly hadn't seen much of the world judging by her cursed curiosity.

But despite all those weaknesses, she was dead set on challenging me, feeding my inner demons.

"Get out. I won't repeat this again." I wasn't known to be patient, clement, or easily entertained. I was most of the time bored, reading through each person's soul with disturbing ease, predicting their reactions and shameless desires.

She averted her gaze to the ground, probably wishing she'd find a way out from this nightmare. From me. After panting breaths, she raised her head and drowned her eyes in mine.

Sweetheart, you're in for a fright.

Her pulse throbbing in her throat, she licked her glossy, sultry mouth, struggling to untie her mask with her delicate hands. My lips pulled into a snarl—she was predictable, after all. Women's beauty had never gotten to me. I wasn't that weak. I knew the reason for their attention was because they wanted a bite of the power I conveyed. If you wanted to rule the underworld, you needed to deliver sins, not consume them—and none of them enraptured me to the point of consumption.

"I was just intrigued by the odor of this flower. I've never smelled anything like it. It's fascinating. There is something special, I just know it, and—" She smiled coyly to herself, her eyes sparkling with joyful infatuation. "I'm a perfumer. I mean, I want to be."

"Really," I hissed ironically.

"Yes. It's my dream. A family legacy in a way." She confided in me, even though I didn't know what gave her the impression I cared about any of this.

Nevertheless, my eyes latched onto her, intrigued. Everything about Ravencliff Manor was the epitome of ugly: from the place itself, to the depraved crowd, to that repulsive corpse flower. But just like the manor, it had a somber history.

A part of my forgotten soul was left in there.

The Devil's Corpse was one of the rarest flowers in the world. No one succeeded in extracting the scent of it without losing its power. All the men I'd employed had been all useless—especially the last one, Eugene Edmond. I'd been told it was rotten, with no hope for transformation. An indomitable spectacle. A mixture of power and monstrousness.

Hope wasn't allowed.

"I'm sorry, I was out of bounds," she added, finishing her discourse.

When she removed her mask and dropped it on the floor, my trousers became immediately tighter. *Well, I'll be damned.* I wasn't expecting her to entice this kind of chemical reaction nor that unwelcome bulge.

Her long, temptress hair waltzed with the draft in my direction, intoxicating me with her seductive perfume of pumpkin pie and something sweeter, perhaps rose. Her brown copper hair, the color between bronze and caramel, tumbling over her breasts was enough to make my muscles stiff.

Her fiery eyes bewitched me, brushing over my skin in a submissive way. She took my silence for punishment, playing the lost doe whilst her physical traits showed her as a predator.

A fantasy coming right from my dreams.

I thought the universe was playing a twisted joke on me.

Only the ugly and corrupt entered those doors.

She wasn't—or if she was, she was the sweetest of the abominations.

In just an instant, that angelic face of hers was a lie I wanted to possess. That grace of her attracted the ugliness of my soul. Her beauty was a curse for every man on Earth. She would burn me if I got closer, but I had the sudden desire to find out what dark compulsions she was hiding.

She was poisonous.

Just like this flower.

The type of woman you either break or worship.

The one you'd build a kingdom for, or make her your slave.

That uncanny duality made me do something I thought I'd never do—ask. "What's your name?" I was convinced the more I learned about her, the more that spell would break. All I had to do was kill the mystery—replace the fantasy with the somber reality.

"Lily Bellerose," she whispered softly with sweet blossom lips.

The niece of an incompetent man had captured my attention. *Lily… Lily… Lily.* She had to be an illusion. An illusion strangely familiar, but at the same time, unattainable. It felt like déjà vu. A memory I'd buried a long time ago was trying to reemerge.

It didn't matter. She was presumably a lie. The impostor swore she had no idea about our past "agreement." But she couldn't be that clueless? Or could she? All I knew was humans were liars, thieves, entrapped in their perversions. We destroyed everything we touched without any chance of salvation. I wondered what sins she would crave? What would make her break?

I needed to tear apart that illusion.

"And you are…" She was afraid to pronounce my name, letting the words linger between her lips.

"What am I?" I edged closer to her, wedging her between the savage flowers.

She glanced back, hoping to find a way out, but she was trapped. I fed on her fear, and as I towered over her, the moonlight illuminated the side of my face. I heard her heavy heartbeat, the terror stabbing her heart and freezing her blood vessels. It pained her to swallow, her pupils dilated, and I knew she had seen it.

Plunging her eyes into mine with a curiosity that would put

her in danger, she met a glimpse of the thorns of my scar hidden behind my mask. Some would say a demon carved half of my face from his imprint. Others, that it was the brand of hell.

I silently cursed myself to have gotten much closer than I should have, and I inched backward.

"They call you the Devil." The way she chose her words carefully showed how blind and naive she was.

I was dreaded. Cruel. Inexorable.

Women dug that in this world. Good girls fell for bad boys, and bad girls liked monsters. But me, I was something else entirely.

I was hell.

And hell was meant to rule alone.

"People call me Witch," she added. It was bold of her to assume we had anything in common.

We didn't belong to the same tale. We were reversed elements.

I was chaos seeking light.

Fire seeking water.

Evil seeking purity.

"Making perfume doesn't necessarily make you a witch." A name is an identity; it's not granted. It's a reputation that is owned and deserved.

"I guess I'm just…" She searched for her words, tugging her lower lip nervously. She glanced over the vines that were climbing over the windows of the greenhouse to gather her strength. "Weird. I'm seeing the world in a different way. I'm more comfortable with flowers than humans sometimes. People don't understand me, but it's what I love. The scent we're attracted to can tell a lot about us… It defines us. It's a form of expression in a way." She spoke with a rare passion, as if she was inhabited by something stronger than her.

Being different is a curse among normality. People have always been afraid of who or what they can't understand. She was right. But she did something wrong by exposing her vulnerability to someone who had the capacity to break her.

Unless I did use her.

The way her stare crept under my skin, with curiosity and sweetness, would make her an unwanted problem. A complication. But my only remaining solution was witchcraft. My family secrets were obscure and hidden in their graves. I'd built an empire where the horror of life collided with the ecstasy of it. I'd succeeded in creating the perfect illusion, a synesthesia of sense, a fusion in quest of the ideal—the final strike was the smell.

Ki shan I Romani—

Adoi san' I chov'hani.

Wherever gypsies go, there the witches are, we know.

Us gypsies had a lot of legends. I wasn't much of a believer, even though I always kept a set of Major Arcana tarot cards. It was the only thing I'd inherited from my mother—the art of divination.

I only needed one card to reveal a person's personality and aspirations. Most of my guests tonight were *The Fool*—they were reckless and in need of an adventure to hell. The weakest ones were *The Lovers*—easily tempted and impressed. Some of the most ambitious businessmen I worked with acted like *The Emperor* while in fact they were a reversed *Wheel of Fortune*—their loss was my gain. *The Hanged Man* was a lost cause I never indulged in business with.

I knew every card. I could read each of their games. But I feared only one card.

I wondered which one she could be?

"Why were you stealing what doesn't belong to you?" The answer was obvious, but I needed to know how far she was willing to go.

"I know I shouldn't have done that. I just want to create a perfume. I need something different and... special." Her voice was trembling, but her determination was stronger than fear. It wasn't courage—no, she wasn't that brave.

My mouth set in a grim line.

It was obsession.

"So you devoted your attention to something ugly, repulsive, and poisonous?" I dropped, dangerous and threatening, while the spikes of the flowers bled the naked skin of her arms when she tried to escape me. The thorns locked her up in their embrace, like a rope keeping her at my mercy.

"There is beauty in the ugly," she replied.

Divine and infernal.

Her own obsession planted a lethal desire in me.

"Lily! Where are you? Lily!" The annoying voice of a man resonated across the garden.

A sharp gasp exhaled through her lips, and I allowed myself to glance at her gracious profile one last time. Then, I disappeared through the dark to head back where I was expected.

There is beauty in the ugly. We'll test that, Lily Bellerose.

After all, this tale isn't how a villain was born.

It's about his rise. His revenge. His obsession.

Chapter 4

Lily

"Where were you?"

Adonis searched for my attention, but I was gobsmacked by what happened earlier at the greenhouse. It was now hidden by the fog after Radcliff's departure, as if the whole place mirrored him. However, his all-male musky scent and obscure aura remained like a somber memory.

All my senses were on hyperalert. I felt more alive than I ever had. The adrenaline rush of the fright that this man emanated impregnated my cells. The fear that rolled down my spine was addictive. Something I couldn't explain had happened.

"Lily? Are you okay?" Adonis asked again, forcing me to regain my perception of reality.

"Yes, everything's fine." I smiled, hiding that my only wish was to go back to that greenhouse. All I had in mind was perfume, but

Adonis left me no choice but to follow him back to the heart of the party.

"Where is your mask, by the way?"

I realized I'd completely forgotten about it, and I doubted Radcliff would give it back to me. How fairy-tale of me to leave a trace behind. "It's inside the greenhouse. Maybe I should—"

"It's okay. Who cares?" He pulled his mask off as well. "There is some crazy shit happening here. There's a guy who juggles with a fucking parrot on his shoulder, while one woman had plastic surgery done to look like the Joconde. I wouldn't be surprised if that freak had a wicked dungeon in the basement."

I laughed at Adonis's gossip while he demonstrated with gestures and sparkling eyes his adoration and somehow jealousy for this show. We were both obsessed with the universe we discovered tonight.

Him, by the bright and festive side.

Me, by a particular man and his cursed flower.

Back inside, I faced an exuberant circus—the overwhelming dancing, the ebbing laughter similar to the sneer of clowns, toasts served by acrobats, the air charged with whiffs of grandiosity, the symphony of the orchestra like a wicked vampire ball. If its owner was the Monster, I certainly was the guinea pig.

"Dance with me?" Adonis's grin was irresistible. Women had their eyes stuck on him. He had the looks and the money, a dangerous combination where just a sign from him would convey their adoration into devotion.

"Are you sure?" A malicious smile on my face, I raised an eyebrow in the direction of the predatory woman next to us. "I think Marie Antoinette over there would enjoy it very much."

"I want to dance with the most beautiful woman in the room." It was needless to talk about how smooth and charming he was. He had the gift of words.

I shook my head sideways. A part of me wanted to hide in a corner for the rest of the night, but lightning struck again. The man who was himself an inferno found his way back to me. At the opposite side of the room, we were back to our staring game, his eyes surrounded by shadows latching onto me.

Freaks among freaks.

It felt like everything was spiraling around us.

Usually, you see the face of a man first. But me, I met the man first. He was incontestably menacing with the power of invisibility. Except for me. My eyes were wide open. I was seeing Radcliff, the glimpse of his impenetrable conflict underneath, not the superficial show he was delivering.

Half ghost. Half monster. What about his humanity?

"Fine, I'll dance with you." I needed to save myself from Radcliff's attempt to capture my soul.

I took Adonis's hand as he led me to the middle of the room, where people were giving themselves lavishly to the pleasures of their bodies, using dancing as the love language of Eros. Adonis seized my waist to press our bodies flush together in an Argentine tango, transporting us to a simpler time.

My dress fluttered against his costume, its movements as light as a veil, unlike the other women's dresses, which looked like circus tents rotating like spinning tops. They formed a barrier in front of Radcliff, sneering and making me feel dizzy. I clung to Adonis, and even his lavender scent couldn't bring me back to normality. My mind played tricks on me. Dresses became clowns. Servers took the shape of skeletons. Laughter became demonic.

I abandoned myself to each note of the dark and enthralling music, taking part in this circus. It was getting harder to breathe. I couldn't escape my mixed feelings. The memory of Radcliff under the moonlight, his scent mixed with the corpse flower filled my lungs, overshadowing the one of Adonis. I spun around, my heart-beat hammering like a volcano about to erupt.

He haunted my mind, overclouding this dance. The craziness from this moment cloaked him to perfection, until he eclipsed this carnival of guests into an invisible fog, and only he and I seemed to remain. I felt as if the dark mirth in his gaze had entrapped me to his carousel, where we were spinning endlessly.

My face became a firestorm; the death in his eyes nestled me in his darkness. My eyebrows dipped, my mind going into delirium, to a point I couldn't tell what was real and what was illusion.

Unsmiling. Unwelcoming. Unyielding Radcliff.

The red hellfire color that tarnished a part of his right eye.

The hint of the disgraceful scar.

The glimpse of the red veins on the sclera of his right eye.

I saw it all.

As fright crept through my spine, Adonis reeled me around. My back was facing his torso, his breath so close to my neck. The hot smoke of his breath was nothing compared to the boiling temperature of my body. I was high on dopamine.

My mind was an exquisite form of self-destruction.

My lips parted, and some strands of my hair fell messily onto my face. A drop of sweat drifted from my collarbone to inside my corset. Captured in the moment, I was compelled by an unknown force to look at the man representing the sins, the chills, and the ugly. His soul was holding the gates of hell when his eyes dipped down and lingered on my body, observing each of my moves and curves.

The strength of his stare was menacing, an intensity that would break anyone. Goose bumps rushed over my naked arms. I couldn't hold his stare any longer; it was like looking directly at burning sunlight. Another drop of sweat slipped.

The dull pain in my chest was a warning I should stop. But I couldn't. The music rose higher. My feet graced the floor seductively in a half circle, Adonis's fingers skimming over my legs.

I was dancing between two men, stuck between terror and arousal.

Caught endlessly in a triangle between the soul and the head.

My head craved the light, the easy, while my soul was governed by a dark obsession. I was a tornado fighting two extremes tempting me toward different sins and desires. The music became a dark lullaby. Each note was a sign of fate to choose a path.

The witch, the devil, and the prince.

Adonis caressed my thighs, raking his fingers into my skin as if he craved to own me, while I watched the chandeliers twirling, the crystals reflecting on the ceiling. He then whirled me around so our bodies could merge again. His fingers trailed over my cheek in a touch that was impure, unlike him. I used to compare his skin tone with the color of a rose, but now he was crimson. Even his scent was different, reddish and stronger with the sweat of the dancing, similar to the sour nuance of rhubarb. He sure reeked of alcohol, but there was something animal about it.

"I want to kiss you," Adonis muttered.

The color of his eyes, usually a turquoise, calm ocean, was submerged by his dilated pupils. A thunderstorm was taking place inside of them.

"You're drunk." I pushed him away gently, dragging my eyes to the floor.

Adonis wasn't used to being refused by women, but I'd never felt for him what I should feel. His scent didn't procure excitement and want. Butterflies never danced inside my belly. Love—that wasn't it.

I wasn't a saint, but intimacy scared me. I'd once explored my body in research for pleasure, but a part of me felt ashamed. I wasn't naive and knew what men awaited from me—my body, my first.

However, the sweetness of a smile was all I could offer, because no one wanted to be inside the soul of a witch.

After all this time, I wanted to convince myself there was more to pure Lily. I had a feeling that a demon inside of me was flourishing, demanding only to reach ecstasy, craving what I'd been warned against.

"Does it matter?" Adonis brushed the strands of my hair away from my face. "You have to admit, we would fit well together. As a prince, I'll make you my princess."

Fairy tales were all about the prince getting his beloved. He fell in love with a glimpse, but did he truly know her soul? Princesses were perfect—a mix of beauty, docility, grace with kindness and courage. Who wouldn't want to be one of them?

My uncle told me once, witches were striving for immortality. I believed they had the power to shake the boundaries of the world. They were the seductresses, lionesses, in control of their own fate, living countless adventures.

Perhaps it wasn't that bad after all to be the villain of the fairy tale.

"You don't know what you're saying right now." I was no longer dancing. A nervous smile crept across my face, and I crossed my arms. I didn't know how to act, conflicted between my friendship with Adonis and a new questioning pondering—what if I was wrong? Adonis could be perfect for me.

"I do. It's you who can't see it." He jerked his head backward and laughed before his cocky grin brought out his dimples. "Open your eyes, princess."

My nose was my vision.

The music of the orchestra stopped abruptly, replaced immediately by the cheers of the crowd. Adonis and I parted. He already had forgotten we ever had that conversation, judging by the way he swallowed another champagne glass. I turned around, hearing someone's heavy steps on the table in front of the imposing gothic windows and velvet curtains.

The man bowed, attracting the attention of everyone to him with a loud hello. He delivered a bright smile to the crowd. He was charismatic, in spite of that fake mole and the emerald wig on his hair. His skin was the color of brown boat orchids, glittering like topaz.

"Ladies and gentlemen, midnight is approaching. If you may follow me to the garden, it's time for the hunt," he exclaimed, taking the duty of the host of the night.

Glancing around the room, I observed Radcliff darting past the guests to escape the social gathering through a dim hallway. Each of his movements was smooth and controlled. I was the only one to see him leave. He was a shadow at his own party, having no problem letting another man have all the spotlight.

I searched for Adonis among the masks and wigs, but he was nowhere to be found. In a rush, everyone gathered at the entrance of the garden with excitement. The guest list smelled of depravation, their perfumes spicy and sugary. Pushed back by the cacophony of the crowd, I couldn't fight my way against them. It was like swimming against the tide. I surrendered, letting myself be carried away until I crossed the elegant parterre and groves of cypress.

I was back at the gothic gates. They were open, leading to the abyss of the forest. Sparkling garlands of light illuminated the path of the night, but it was nonetheless a scary spectacle.

The only sign of life was miles away.

We were alone.

I was alone.

Fortunately—or so I thought—the crowd walked away from the somber forest to edge toward the back of the manor. I followed them, panic sending a stream of frozen air through my spine. With an abrupt halt, they all stopped, and I dared to look up.

I blinked twice.

The sight in front of me was terrifying and somehow cryptic.

A deathly stillness possessed me, wondering if Radcliff wasn't a sorcerer with twisted tricks in his hat.

A maze.

The hedges of the yew trees formed a prison high enough that no one could dare to see what was over them. They were cut with a square top. In the center, as bait, a single light was attached to the top of an oak tree. It was a trap in the midst of darkness.

It looked bigger than any other maze. Dangerous. Unfriendly. It sent the clear message that once you entered, your fate was sealed.

"For the welcomers, here are the rules. Twelve of you have been offered a ribbon, the different colors representing the twelve strikes of midnight. You'll be the lucky players of tonight. The chosen ones. Please step out, don't be shy," the strange man announced with enthusiasm.

The eleven chosen giggled with delirium. They stood proudly near the man acting as host, their eyes beaming at the guests with vainglory. I untied the black satin ribbon on my wrist, trying to fist it inside my palm, having no desire to take part in this circus.

But he saw me. "You. Come here."

The extroverted man pointed his finger at me, a malicious smile stretching on his face. He took another sip of his flask, leaning backward like a drunken pirate. He winked at me before he dipped into a curtsy and offered me his hand. Reluctantly, I cursed him inside when I let myself get taken next to the rest of the chosen.

"We have our hunted for the night. Now, all we need are our hunters."

The howling wind whipped through the tree branches of the maze, a frozen breath coming out of the entrance. The squall came over us, delivering its menacing threat.

I glared around me. Who were those people? They whistled

impatiently. I couldn't possibly understand the appeal of this game. I was probably one of the youngest people here. The rare women who could have been my age wore so much makeup and looked so seductive that it was impossible to tell they were barely legal. How could a chase be attractive for grown-ups?

"Excuse me—hunted?" I asked with a sudden confidence that vanished the second those words came through my mouth, giving way to a shrieking panic. Irritation rushed through my veins. I hadn't signed up to be part of a vicious game.

"Yes, darling." His eyes flickered with a salacious expression that meant *up to no good*, a devilish smile on his face. He stepped toward me, waltzing his hands to the tempo of the background music of Parov Stelar like a drunken magician—a poor imitation of Jack Sparrow, if you asked me. "If you survive your hunter by protecting your ribbon until the horn thunders and escaping the maze, you win. But if you don't succeed either of them… you'll experience the rest of the night with extreme pleasure or… suffering."

I swallowed. The crowd cackled with macabre laughter. This was far from the games you played as kids. It was a game of cat and mouse crossed with a twisted version of spin the bottle. Because here, I'd have to stay locked down with a bigger monster and with someone wanting to steal more than a kiss from me.

"Should I add, many players remain stuck inside the maze. It is almost impossible to get out of it, and no one will help you out," the host continued, his gaze fixed on mine. "You're on your own. Hunters, take place in front of your matching ribbon."

In an instant, boyfriends and girlfriends started to kiss heavily, while some duos screamed of a kinky imbalance of power. I stood alone under the stars, waiting for Adonis to appear—after all, he was my date and the only person I trusted here.

I entangled my fingers together, a bad feeling invading me. I felt the heavy, judging gazes of the guests on me and their whispers sending me venom. They wanted to play, and I was slowing them down. I screamed silently, a countless number of times, calling out for Adonis.

But he never came.

I wanted to leave. I could have left. I didn't. Instead, I let the adrenaline, the apprehension of what came next, consume my cells.

The crowd parted unexpectedly, as the water did in front of their prophet. My throat dried, and I ran out of air, experiencing this moment in slow motion. All I could see was the shadow of a man ambling like an elegant panther in my direction. The smoke was hiding his face, but each of his steps was determined, leaving an imprint on the grass.

He had the scariest confidence, a magnetism that was unlike any other. But what gave him away was that musky, dangerous scent that magnified his darkness. He wore it like a smokey wood wedged into the depths of hell. A burning coal that froze your veins if you got closer. A fatal breath he'd take from you at nightfall inside a forest of scars.

Radcliff, the Devil, was my hunter.

Chapter 5

Lily

I kept my head down, praying that my lips wouldn't shake. Everything became a tormenting silence as if Radcliff had sucked the life out of the garden, stealing all the oxygen.

His somber aura melted mine to the point each of my fibers wanted to take root underneath the earth. He stopped near me, and the hair on my skin raised alert, reacting to him like a magnet. He hid the moonlight by his imposing size, his shadow sinking me into the obscurity.

This had to be a nightmare. At any moment, I would wake up. This theory crumbled to ashes when I pinched myself, and a shout of pain pierced me. It was a nightmare. A real one. The kind I wouldn't wake up from.

I exhaled, the mist from my mouth vaporizing into the wintry air, dancing toward the road of freedom. Carefully and slowly, I looked heavenward to Radcliff. The smoke was long gone, and our gazes were firmly set on each other. His eyes held magic and mystery, reminding me of a gothic flower. A purple calla lily.

"Oh, sweet virgin is gonna be eaten by the big bad wolf," the woman next to me whispered to her hunter, interrupting my thoughts.

I turned to face her, and through her black lace mask, she raised an eyebrow at me before chortling. I interpreted this gesture as a way to let me know it was her intention that I listened. Her emerald eyes gleamed with… jealousy? Her hair, dark and curly, reminded me of the snakes of Medusa. She eyed my hunter with an interrogative look, but I could still feel Radcliff's cold stare on me.

"Thirty minutes in hell or in heaven. At the horn, hunted… run. May you escape your fate!" The eccentric speaker blew into the horn, making it thunder for the other eleven hunted to race, bolt, and gallop in the direction of the maze.

But the Devil and I remained like stones at the witching hour.

The hunters started their chase, but the guests' elation was contained, waiting eagerly for Radcliff to make his move, to deliver them the spectacle they had been craving.

"If I were you, I'd run," Radcliff dropped from his mouth, hard and thin, with no vestige of sympathy.

There was no escape. The wind whistled a dark melody at the entrance to the maze, as if the ghosts had taken over the party. Sometimes, distant shrieks resurfaced. My heart pounded; I was surrounded on each side. I opted for the lesser evil and gathered my courage in a shaky exhale.

The time had come.

I sprinted like a chased doe being hunted down into the wild prison, my legs taking control of my brain.

I ran with all the blood my heart was pumping.

I ran with all the air in my lungs.

I ran because I didn't need to see him riding on a black chariot to know that hell was chasing after me.

Inside the maze, panic rushed through my veins. The concentric rings seemed infinite with patterns that all looked similar. I stumbled upon countless dead ends, my only wish to make this hunt stop. The smell of pine, leather, and fresh rain gave a dramatic turn to this place, a morbid atmosphere. I was trapped, engulfing myself in a knot impossible to untie. With layer after layer of pathways, finding the end was impossible.

My feet hit a rock abruptly, and I tumbled over the wet grass. My pure as white dress was soiled with dirt. I stood up, ignoring the bruising on my knee. I had to move on, even if the hostile nature was tearing my dress apart, scarring it until the beauty of it no longer existed.

I swore I could hear the demon voices calling my name through the bushes of trees; I sensed their presence in the fog. I kept an eye on the lighted oak tree in the center. I had to reach it. Each tunnel felt like hell was chasing after me, gaining ground on me every minute.

My hair was wet, pieces of grass stuck on the lengths, from my fall and the running. I found myself stuck between paths, and I stopped to catch my breath. I wasn't that far from finding the exit, but I was incapable of making a decision. I was too deep in the maze to back down, and no one would rescue me. My only certitude was that I needed to get closer to the light, even if it was where everyone would be. I wouldn't make it in the darkness.

I took the path to the right. Fleeing through it, I met some players kissing heavily against the trees. The dresses of the women were lifted up, their moans melding with the groaning of the men. Some of them were tied up, their hands on the rope tightened on the branch, their breasts offered in view of anyone. Sometimes, the roles were reversed. They giggled with appetency like demons owning the night. What was I doing here?

I passed by them, anxiety consuming me. My courage vanished in the wake of my fear. My forehead creased, my eyes begging for this night to end. I was ready to admit defeat. The tree branches terrorized me into a gloomy lullaby. The players' moans of pleasure crept through my spine. The cold air smelled like death itself.

I ran, having no idea where I was going until I arrived at the promised land. The center, where the light stood on top of an oak tree. I knew I was exposed under the light, but the monster you can see is easier to beat. I curled up on myself, waiting like an abandoned child. I counted the seconds in the hope of making the trembling of my body stop. *One. Two. Th*—

"Lily," a low breath tinged with menace resounded.

I bolted away from the tree in panic, my skin bristling. My eyes frantically searched the area, having a mind of their own until they stopped at the shadow in front of me.

I was facing a stern and pitiless Radcliff.

The Unseen.

The Wealthy One.

The Giver of Wealth.

"What's the goal of this? Why are you doing this?" I lost control of my voice in a high-pitched scream.

He didn't reply, scrutinizing me with a deadly stillness.

I took a step back when his foot cracked the dead branches on the ground. We stalked in circles around the tree in a murky dance. A silent duel, like wild animals observing the foreigner. His hands in his pockets, Radcliff stood upright and ruthless. He had a rare— yet terrifying—elegance, as if he were coming from another time. Me, on the contrary, I was a mess. Weak and vulnerable. A part of my soul had been corrupted tonight, rotten to the core.

"People like to play games." His lips turned cruel at the corners.

He waltzed his fingers through the fresh air, like one would do listening to a classical masterpiece. He then inhaled his surroundings as if it were the most sumptuous of perfumes. Radcliff was in his element, becoming one with the scary and the madness. The night and the wicked.

"They like the prospect of winning while some others enjoy losing to someone so they can free their desires without judgment," he continued in a cold, detached tone, as if he was biased by humans. The curse of a man who has seen it all—the atrocity and the corruption, the lowest points of humanity. To the point, he must have erased goodness from his heart.

"Do you?" I asked, my pitch unsure and soft.

He loomed slowly toward me, each of his steps making my heart leap in my throat. I was undeniably scared of that man.

Not by whatever repulsive appearance he might have, no.

Not by whatever gossip I heard, no.

I was scared of that bond we both felt. That life-threatening fascination.

"Do you play?" I repeated, hoping he'd stop.

"No, I just deliver."

But he played tonight with me. All night we had played. "Why, then? What do you expect?"

In a thunderclap, I was pinned against the tree, caged between Radcliff's arms. His soul trapped me—I was unable to escape. My heart seemed to have stopped, the blood running through my veins slowing down its course to freeze. His dark essence melted with my sweet one, intoxicating each other in a battle of power.

He felt it, that stirring combination.

Opposite forces, equally strong, befuddling us.

"This is what you expect, then?" My mouth shook when I felt his fingers skimming the length of my arm to descend to my palm in search of the ribbon.

As if he had the power to take or revive life, his touch on my bare skin resurrected my heartbeat, which was now hammering at full speed. Instinctively, I pulled both of my hands up. A pointless act since he was much taller than me.

"No. I don't want your body... Witch." He cuffed my hands with his, towering dangerously over me.

His grip was firm and cold as stone. An iron fist that could break me at any moment. I wanted to close my eyes to blind myself, but it'd only alert the rest of my senses. I searched for any sign of humanity and mercy, trying to get a glimpse of the man behind the Devil's mask, but he gave me nothing.

Instead, he clutched my waist with his calloused hand with a dominant and directive touch. However, it wasn't to merge our bodies together. The opposite—it was to keep our bodies apart. I was stuck against the tree while the veins and muscles of his hand and forearm tensed, acting like a shield between us.

His body betrayed him.

A dilemma was rising inside of him.

It was a devious test.

He expected my fear, repulsion, and weakness.

But I'd give him my strength. "What do you want, then?"

He let go of his hand on my waist before setting his palm on the tree trunk near my head. Some bark fell to the ground at his contact and in its descent transformed itself into particles of ashes. I craned my neck, our eyes boring into each other. He darted his tongue out and wet his full lips. I didn't move. In nature, when prey debates with herself, it stirs up the predator even more.

"Your soul."

I gasped. No men have ever chased after my soul. They chased after my appearance or the carnal pleasure. They had never been interested in digging deeper, to my thoughts or my drive.

But this man was the Devil.

He was undeniably more frightening than any other man I'd met, for a reason I completely ignored until now.

He wanted my soul.

Every piece, until devotion and ownership.

The horn sounded, and he stole the ribbon from my fingers. He pulled away from the tree, so I could find my breath again. Something was missing inside of me, as if he had stolen a piece of me or awakened a silent hole that needed to be fed.

He hid the ribbon inside his vest pocket in one swift move and tightened his costume. Sounds of laughter rang out, the crowd dispersing in the maze.

"Take three right turns. Then, turn to the left." He slowly shifted his head toward the exit, then locked his eyes firmly on me. "You don't want to stay for what happens next."

That was an order I took gladly. "Thank you."

I fled from the phantom, following his instructions. I escaped the maze and that somber night where people worshipped darkness rather than light.

But one thing was for sure. I would never be able to escape how I felt that night.

Nor that man.

I had to think fast. I wasn't out of the woods. I didn't have time to dwell on what had just happened as I searched for Adonis in the midst of the decaying air and stifling atmosphere. He was nowhere to be found. The wailing sounds ghosting through the trees tried to catch up to me. I thought strategically to avoid the guests and ran in the direction of the greenhouse, hoping to find my mask.

The sparkling light still illuminated the inside. I rushed to it and wrenched the door open, feeling safe for a moment. I didn't let myself catch my breath; I had to move forward if I wanted to get out of here. I grabbed my soiled mask on the floor, and suddenly, the lights switched off.

I was stuck in the middle of the darkness. Oblivion. The nothing.

I panicked, my biggest fear coming to life. I turned around abruptly, hearing a knocking sound. Someone had locked me up inside. *No.* I stormed at the door, seeing only a silhouette leaving in the distance.

"Help!" I shrieked. "Please, help!"

I screamed, but no one heard my distress. I was trapped. I slammed the windows with my fists, imploring, "Please, I need help. Can someone hear me?"

The music was too loud, leaping above my voice. I hit the door until my fists bled, controlled by the primal instinct of fear to escape. I could smell the metallic tang of my blood, leaving a bitter taste in my throat. I fidgeted around every corner of the greenhouse, trying to break the windows. Objects smashed on the ground, and I trampled everything in my path.

I cried, yelled, begged, my invisible demons reaching out to me. I was seeing them.

The sisters.

The Institute for Young Ladies.

The place where I grew up that haunted my nightmares.

But this time… no one was here.

14 years ago

Curled up on myself on the grass, I prayed for the lullaby to stop. I covered my ears with my palms, my mouth tasting earthy.

"Wet grass. Rain. Disgusting mint," I listed the smells around me in a whisper. *Again.* "Wet grass. Rain. Dis—"

Their voices were too loud. I couldn't focus nor escape the mean girls from the orphanage. They held each other's hands, spinning in a circle around me like she-demons encircling me like a prison of torment.

Beware of the Witch.

Removing petals of flowers at early bloom,

She's gifted with a curse.

Floral, oriental, woody, fresh, scents have no secrets for her.

Beware of the Witch.

She'll put a spell on you.

Sweet and innocent, but yet poisonous.

A dark secret she's hiding.

Beware of the Witch.

Because to every Witch, there is a Devil.

They repeated it in a symphony, and no one cared that they were blaspheming the Institute of Young Ladies.

"It's not true," I sobbed, and tightened my fists before sinking them in the dirt.

Tears stung my eyes. I smashed the flowers, making them bleed and hurting my heart at the same time. *Stop crying, Lily.* I wouldn't be reduced to a creature.

I was stronger than that.

Mom told me with my beauty, I'd make friends. She told me with my gift, I'd inspire. But she never imagined it'd cause me only pain. They wanted to take my belongings, my life, my beauty away. And they could. They could take everything but my essence.

I stood up, holding on to what was left of my pride with my uniform covered in mud. Mom wasn't of this world anymore, but Uncle would come to pick me up soon. It was temporary, he said. On holidays, I'd be with him. I just needed to hold on a bit longer.

The sisters raced in our direction, breaking the circle to join me. For them, I was a spoiled child with vanity for sin. Vain and too proud, they called me. The other girls remained silent, a wicked self-satisfied smile on their faces. *I hate them.*

"It's her." One pointed her finger at me as the others followed.

Mother Anne grabbed my arm harshly to force me to go once again to the place of my nightmares for my punishment. Fighting was useless. We walked into the lifeless hallway, my tears not stopping.

"Conceited girl, you need to learn how to behave," she yelled before throwing me into what felt like a cell.

It was a cold room with stone walls where at night you'd freeze sleeping on the floor mattress. It had no lights. That place was meant to break our spirit.

"Please don't leave me alone here. I did nothing wrong!" I cried and begged so many times, but they were all pitiless.

"You're not alone." She was right. I was in hell, surrounded by demons. "You're a sinner who deserves to be here. You need to stop causing problems, and you'll learn how to behave the hard way. It's for your own good, *precious* child."

She locked the door behind her, leaving me with my horrors. I wished nothing of me remained in this world. The room was without scent but for the smell of chaos and despair.

My mom used to say we all had a guardian angel. So every night, I prayed that mine would save me. But instead, all I saw were monsters in the night. There were no scented candles to calm me down nor to protect me from them.

The hours passed. I felt my skin turning blue, my lips drying, and my essence vanishing. I was a flower born in the wrong field, and I was fading, losing each of my petals.

I thought my mind was playing tricks on me when I heard footsteps behind my door.

"Please..." I was so chilled with terror that even my voice shivered.

I inhaled the scent. Mostly strong and powerful, it had a touch of vanilla. The one carried on a pirate boat that had landed on a tropical island where men battled with swords and women wore corsets.

The scent somehow smelled masculine, even though it wasn't possible. No boys were allowed here. Apart from the Father, who was the director of the Institute for Young Ladies. All I knew was that it appeased me, transporting me to an adventure of a lifetime.

My guardian angel had come.

The stranger slid a bar of candy from under the door—only privileged children had those.

"How did you find it?"

My guardian angel remained silent.

"What's your name?" I asked, ripping the candy bar's paper open to eat it.

He or she started to leave before I implored, "Please. Stay. We don't have to talk."

The footsteps stopped, and my companion sat behind my door.

My guardian angel stayed silently by my side, that day, and the many others to come. Protecting me by watching over me, being my hope. Until that day.

The day when my guardian angel abandoned me.

Forever.

Chapter 6

Radcliff

I exhaled sharply, watching the last car leave through the gothic gates—with its two passengers standing and raising their arms above the convertible, continuing a madness of their own. That shitshow was finally over. I couldn't handle any more social interactions with any of my guests. They were just useless pawns, thinking their blood made them royals or, even more delusional, gods. Little did they know, their cravings for fame, power, and lust enslaved them to me.

At 6 a.m. sharp, the cleaning team invaded my domain to erase any traces of the New Year's Eve extravaganza before noon.

The first rays of sun peeked through the gardens, the smoke of my cigar fogging the light. That was my cue to go. I sank deeper into my courtyard, having no desire to be disturbed nor to see more of those grey uniforms. They contemplated my property as if it was some touristic haunted house, imagining they'd be the chosen one to have a look at the monstrous Devil. *Imbeciles.*

My eyes darted to the greenhouse, paused, then shifted again. *What the actual fuck.*

The transparent windows let me glimpse the potting soil that was spilled on the ground, alongside crushed flowers that had been thrown all over. Pots were broken. Saying that it was a bloody mess was an understatement.

In a sudden mood for wrath, I stubbed my cigar on the floor before tamping down my irritation, unclenching my fist. I strode closer. The repellant smell was warning enough to scream of every shade of forbidden.

The greenhouse was locked from the outside, but that wasn't all. With an icy coldness, I flung the door open in a sharp movement, my lips pursed together. In the middle of the chaotic scenery, an angel fallen from heaven was huddled on the paving stones.

Lily. She slept on her side, her spine curved, pulling her legs close to her frigid body. Her dress was tarnished by soil, small cuts inked on her skin as a somber memory of the night of terror she had passed. Her lips were a crimson purple, similar to the Devil's Corpse's bewitching color. The memory of her tears remained on her face. Her makeup was nonexistent, washed away with the fright.

But my attention remained on her savage bronze-copper hair. It was freed, flowers stuck inside it like wild lianas shielding her from the outside world. Sunrise illuminated her face in a vibrant glow. A golden tunnel in the midst of the darkness.

She was a flower goddess.

She screamed of misery and weakness—everything I loathed in anyone else. And yet, it made her beautiful. My nostrils flared. I didn't feel pity for her. On the contrary, I enjoyed the sight of her at my mercy. My lips pressed into a thin line, and a muscle in my jaw clenched. A sudden desire to make whoever was responsible for her state pay pierced my nonexistent heart.

I shouldn't care.

I didn't care.

I would not care.

That little witch had put a spell on me, compelling me to look over her in silence. An achievement no woman had succeeded before her. In her distress, she had planted dark thoughts in me. As if Eros had struck me with one of his stupid arrows, transforming me into a sexually frustrated beast. I yearned to possess her soul, to show her my hell.

I was hell-bent on keeping her.

Imprisoning her with me.

Kidnapping her from her world.

She made me reconsider all my rules. I couldn't be infatuated with her. I wasn't capable of such feelings. Lily was supposed to be gone from my life after the chase. She was a destructive illusion. But that flower goddess awoke the villain in me that wanted to be fed.

The right and only choice was to turn back. I sent a text message to Hugo, asking him to wake her up. After all, it was his job to play the host, not mine. I stalked toward the door, determined to get back inside the peace of my manor. But as I grabbed the handle, an invisible force prevented me from moving forward.

To hell. To fucking hell.

I bit back the fresh swell of irritation growing inside of me, removing my four-thousand-euro tailored suit jacket. I walked back to her, the sound of my footsteps echoing on the floor.

Flames of disapproval licked through me when I laid down the jacket on her naked skin. I tucked her in like a precious jewel. The darkness of my eyes caught her too-perfect face one last time before I disappeared from the greenhouse.

Rushing outside, I flexed my fingers in a sharp movement. The sun behind my back, I entered the murky obscurity of my manor, calling that impostor Eugene Edmond.

"Mr. Radcliff, I—"

"I'm keeping her."

I hung up.

After all, she didn't deserve a prick like him. He was unworthy of her.

I would have thought that I was saving her, but I was not.

I was worse than any other man on Earth.

I was the Devil, after all.

Chapter 7

Lily

A feeling of warmth invaded my core, breaking through the icy obscurity of last night. Through my closed eyelids, a soft white-gold light wrestled to illuminate the abyss of my dreams. Hope surged through my veins when I slowly opened my eyes, facing the wintry sun. My gaze was blurry at first; I had to adjust my sight to distinguish where I was.

I swept my eyes to the corpse flower. It seemed she had been watching over me. Her petals, crimsoned in venous blood, had blossomed as soft as roses. The thorns, as sharp as razor blades, shone in the sun, and the heavy patchouli filled my nostrils. Under this visual poetry, the flashbacks of last night blasted through my core in a rush.

New Year's Eve.

Radcliff.

The hunt.

I had a taste of another world where magic met witchcraft, where addiction met ecstasy, where my own obsession infused in my body in a terrifying elixir. I couldn't escape Radcliff; his image was impregnated in each of my chills.

My sore body straightened before something slid off my shoulders. My eyes flickered over the jet-black jacket set down on my legs. I grazed the material with my nails. It looked expensive. I brought it closer to my nose, picking up the notes. *Sandalwood*. With a hint of a leather scent coming from tobacco. My throat dried, remembering to whom this essence belonged.

Radcliff.

Radcliff had been here. A cloud of steam escaped my lips, the realization of it sweltering my insides despite the iciness of my frightened body.

I blanched, hearing a barking. Turning around, I took sight of a little black dog standing behind me. Probably a female, judging by her feminine, brown, shimmering eyes filled with kindness that would appease any human's soul. She was hiding in the crushed flowers, mingling with them, her tail moving joyfully.

"Come here." I bent down, crouching in front of her to invite her into my arms.

When she rushed toward me with enthusiasm, my heart broke and shattered into pieces. She was a stray dog, with one of her front legs missing. And yet, she ran fiercely, ignoring her handicap. She snuggled against my legs, and I scooped the little warrior into my arms.

"What's your name? You're so pretty."

The dog licked my face, making me giggle. She was one of the happiest animals I'd ever met, not having one ounce of aggression inside of her.

"Her name's Cerba. She's Radcliff's dog," a masculine voice echoed.

Feeling startled, I whirled around to stare at the man behind me. I recognized him instantly. He was the one who'd acted as host at Radcliff's party. The man wrinkled his nose, not fully stepping inside the greenhouse—probably repulsed by the corpse flower's odor.

He was dressed in an emerald velvet suit that screamed of formality, a smug smile painted on his face when I shifted my gaze between Cerba and him, not believing that inhuman Radcliff had a dog.

"Oh—it's a beautiful name." I stood up, folding my arms on my chest. "I'm sorry, I didn't mean to sleep here." Someone had locked me inside—deliberately or not—and here I was apologizing for a fate I wished I had never experienced.

I became aware of the massacre I had done inside the greenhouse in a glance that squeezed my heart. "Nor do all that."

"I'm not the one you should apologize to," he sneered.

"Who are you?"

"I'm here on behalf of Mr. Radcliff." His name shot through me like a massive flood of adrenaline, my wild heart galloping like a fleeing horse. "Looks like you made quite an impression on him," he joked, his gaze homing in on my soiled dress.

"I don't understand." If there was any impression I'd have made on that man, I didn't think it would be him pitying me. "Why didn't he bother to come to me, then? I know he was here. That's his jacket, right?" I gunned my eyes at the man, but he didn't seem slightly deterred by it.

"I like you." My interlocutor didn't bother to hide his amusement. He gave me a sinful smirk as if he had bet on my reaction. "I'm the person he sends to represent him during public events, social interactions etc.—you get the drill. He's a busy man. And as for the other why, I assume you heard the rumors."

What was behind the Devil's mask? This question circled my mind. I had to ask. "Is it true?"

"That's not my story to tell, *doudou*."

I snapped my brows together, and facing my incomprehension, he added, "It means darling in Creole."

At this point, *doudou* couldn't be worse than my other pet names. His eyes shined with mirth, and I decided it was best if I went straight to the point. I suppressed a shiver and demanded, "I would like to go home, but I don't have my phone, and my ride probably left last night."

"Your uncle should arrive soon." He paused. "But you should brace yourself."

"What do you mean?" My eyes went round, and my face was blank.

The man ignored my reaction and was on his way to leave until I called him out. "Wait! What's your name?" Like that seemed a relevant time to ask.

"Hugo."

I bored my eyes into his. Where I grew up, I learned how to differentiate the good from the bad, the lies from the truth. "Hugo, tell me… What kind of man is Radcliff?" He remained silent under my forceful stare. "Would you advise someone you love to get involved with him?"

Truth was, I had no idea why I had such a morbid fascination for him. He screamed of corruption and of the darkest shades of danger. He was nothing I aspired to be—but he had what I aspired to create. Maybe that was all it was about.

"As I said, your uncle should be here any minute." He nipped toward the door, Cerba following after him. While I interpreted his silence as answer enough, he then reeled around to face me. "Radcliff is a complicated man… but he isn't a monster. At least, I don't think so."

A soft smile stretched on his lips, and he closed the door behind him. Alone inside the greenhouse, I gazed upon the manor and its savage nature. In the daylight, it looked different. It was deserted, similar to a ghost town. A gloomy mystery erased from the memory of the earth. The irony of it was that Radcliff reflected the same duality as his manor. Half monster. Half phantom.

I wasn't sure if my brain had filled the silence with the symphony of the waves crashing on the hard rocks or if it was real. Focusing on it, it looked like an invitation to jump into darkness. An entrance to the abyss.

The noise of the ocean disappeared when the gates groaned, opening slowly, like a cry for help, as if the tears of the gods were welcoming its guest. My uncle's car was arriving, driving past the long gravel road. My heart took possession of my legs, and I ran forward to the entrance, forgetting my heels in a rush.

"Uncle!" I yelled, sprinting through the grass barefoot. "I'm so happy that you're here!"

My uncle got out of our old car with a fixed smile that melted into twisted, quivering lips, and the color drained out of his face. He went to the trunk to take out two suitcases. Hugo arrived from behind me, assisting him in a dead silence.

"Uncle, what's happening?" Panic flared in my eyes.

He acted as if I was nonexistent. He didn't shoot me one glance. Didn't speak one word. His movements were mechanical, orchestrated.

Hugo carried the luggage in the direction of the manor. Anxiety eclipsed all my rational thoughts that it was too late before I noticed the gate had shut behind him, separating me from my uncle like a prison wall.

"I'm so sorry, my Lily," Eugene's frail voice echoed like a stab in my heart.

"What—What's the meaning of this?" Fear gripped my throat, my eyes darting between him and Hugo, who remained like a statue a couple of meters away.

"Listen to me." My uncle passed his hands through the bars

of the gate to hold mine, sadness clouding his features. "Do you remember that I came to the manor a couple of times?" I nodded, fighting back tears. "Well, I was working for Mr. Radcliff all this time. I promised I'd do something for him and I… I failed, and I'm in debt to him. You have to help me and stay in the manor to… replace me."

"What!" I screamed, pulling my hands away from him instinctively. "What are you talking about, Eugene?"

"Lily, please," he begged. "I know you can do this. Everything will be fine. You're capable of everything. I'm so sorry, my darling. But in some ways, you'll have everything you ever dreamed of. It's for the best if—"

"For the best?" I shouted. "Why are you telling me all of this now? It doesn't make sense!"

"I wanted to tell you sooner, but I couldn't." *You just couldn't face me.* "It's more complicated than you think, but I have faith in you."

"You're abandoning me! I don't understand what you're saying! Just—don't leave."

"Lily," he stuttered, his mouth shaking as he sniffed. "This is an opportunity for you. I promise. I'm sorry."

Stop lying, Uncle.

"No, no, no," I implored, shaking the bars violently when Uncle Eugene headed back to his car. "Don't abandon me! Don't leave me."

"Be strong for your mother."

My eyes begged to swim with tears, but nothing remained inside of me. I glared at my uncle disappearing through the path and not turning back. He had left me with an uncertain fate he was so eager to get rid of. I'd never seen Uncle Eugene this terrified before, to the point of throwing me out of my current life.

The air thrust itself in and out of my mouth. I refused to believe my uncle could abandon me. He had his reasons. Reasons I needed to find out. *Be strong for your mother.* I took the choice of trusting him one last time.

"The housekeeper will show you inside. I'll take care of your luggage," Hugo added, gesturing to follow him back to the manor.

"What does Radcliff want with me? What did he ask my uncle to do?" I swallowed the anger thrumming through my veins, like a silent volcano about to spring to life.

"He'll explain everything to you tonight, once you settle in." My gaze slithered across my body, imagining all the possible outcomes. "Not that." Hugo shook his head and put his hand up, as if the idea of Radcliff wanting to have sex with me was unimaginable.

I followed Hugo reluctantly through the imposing entrance doors without a word. The gurgling croaks of the ravens filled the silence as if they were the bearers of a bad omen. Inside the manor, the madness of New Year's was long gone. From the main hall to the big corridors, nothing was warm and inviting. Everything was somber with dark curtains that hid any light from entering by covering the big ancient gothic windows.

I faced who I imagined to be the butler and the housekeeper of the house. Both at an older age, they'd probably worked here for decades. They stood like gargoyles in front of me in their black-and-white uniforms, their eyes scrutinizing me.

"Good morning." I waved hello, uncomfortable by the gloomy atmosphere—it was like attending a funeral.

"Mr. and Mrs. Walton took a vow of silence. They won't reply to you," Hugo informed me, passing us with my suitcases.

The old lady gave me a frigid smile and showed me the way. I stalked behind her, sinking into the insanely big mansion, a creepy feeling hissing through my core. The sound of her heels echoed on the floor. The manor smelled of horror haunting tales that you narrate around a campfire—oakmoss, clove leaf and amber.

We headed upstairs, passing through the countless corridors, a cold shiver never leaving my back. In the northeast hallway, artwork that probably cost more than what I could possibly make in two years hung on the wall. One symbolized Dante's Inferno, while the others represented the fall of man, the damned, and the descent of hell. With that infernal series hung a portrait of a child.

He was approximately twelve years old, with a rare sadness for a boy of that age. His face was white as death, cold as stone, with eyes that asked for salvation. His raven-black hair was pulled back, glossy lips twitching backward in disapproval, thick eyebrows pinched. His chin was tilted up in an elegant way. The child was the perfect mixture between beautiful and haunted. An old soul, a boy who'd seen it all.

I jumped abruptly, hearing the cracking noise of the door the housekeeper just opened. She stood in front, crossing her hands in front of her belly, and waited like a royal guard. I guess this was my bedroom.

"Thank you," I said, concealing my despair with a warm smile.

She bowed before taking her leave.

I sucked in a deep breath and pushed the door wide. The only light in the bedroom came from a slit between the heavy velvet curtains at the windows. I rushed to them, the feeble brightness giving me the creeps. Once I opened the curtains, I could distinguish perhaps one of the most beautiful views of the manor from my dusty marble balcony. In an occult landscape, the hostile cliff, the tormented ocean, and the forest gave me an incredible show.

I reeled around, creeping closer to see the opulent and sensual king-size bed with crimson satin sheets. Small lamps sat on nightstands on each side of the bed. Fresh towels were placed on the wooden desk before I noticed the confidentiality agreement lying upon it. Despite the fact that the room looked creepy, surrounded with shadows, I was fine.

Because once again, I buried my feelings inside my brain.

"Hello?" My thin voice echoed through the walls.

No replies.

Coming down the creaky stairs, the only noise I heard was from the cold wind scouring the manor like a spirit wanting to escape.

I couldn't be kept in the blur any longer and made the decision to confront Radcliff. I had washed away all visible traces of what had happened during the past twenty-four hours through the shower. My wet hair brushed against my bordeaux dress that clung to my form perfectly. I wore it with pride; it gave me strength since it had belonged to my mother.

The hallway was huge with a high ceiling, and yet a part of me felt crowded and small passing through it. I turned from side to side, feeling constantly stared at. It was too deserted. Too silent. I had the signed confidentiality agreement in my hand, which basically stated I wouldn't share any pictures or information relating to Ravencliff Manor nor Radcliff. It was my main reason to come back downstairs.

I arrived in the living room, where tufted leather sofas and armchairs stood alongside tapestries, antiques, and an old library. The crystal chandeliers touched in a shrill noise. The flames in the fireplace crackled, seeming even louder as my gaze moved up to the mantel.

That was where I found him. The man belonging to the under-world. Facing him again made each fiber of my body twist in angst, even though his back was turned to me. His stygian suit clung tight to his massive muscles. Cerba sat at her owner's feet; if she had noticed me, she remained motionless, like a guard dog awaiting orders from its master.

Radcliff's black shadow stretched up the wall under the burning light of the flames. I was under the impression his shadow was blanketing the room, constantly moving. It was bigger than he was. Scarier as the Devil's shadow. Inhuman somehow.

Neither of us spoke until I decided to break the silence. "I signed your agreement."

I threw the pieces of paper on the wooden table next to us. The loud sound of pages whipping made Cerba strain an ear. She waved her tail in my direction, probably wanting to play.

"She likes you. Surprising since she usually doesn't like anyone." Radcliff looked down at Cerba, his hair hiding his profile as she gave him soft eyes.

"What happened to her?" I countered, since we weren't speaking about the matter at hand.

"I found her like that. A hit-and-run car left her almost dead years ago, and her owner ignored her existence," he said coldly, like a man used to cruelty. His hand clutched the top of the fireplace and he leaned closer to the flames. "I cursed her with me."

In other words, he had saved her, and a man who rescued a dog couldn't be evil. Another part of Radcliff had to lurk there—something darker that spoke of tragedy, hidden underneath his impenetrable mask. I was convinced villains had hearts. We all had a weakness, someone we loved. A possibility of redemption. Sometimes, all we need is someone to make us remember our humanity.

"That's kind of you."

"There is nothing such as kindness." His cynical tone blew me away.

"You're wrong."

"You're naive," he quipped back.

"Anyway, can you at least explain to me what I am doing here."

He remained silent, his back still facing me. I inched toward him carefully, my heart pounding in my throat. With every step I took, I felt like roots were holding me back. He cracked his knuckles, and I stopped there.

Nervously, I moistened my dry lips and asked, "Can I see you?"

My breath grew thin and ragged. I was already regretting my

question. My stomach contracted into a tight ball, seeing him turn slowly toward me. My skin grew clammy, and I felt myself becoming chalk white the moment he revealed himself to me for the first time. I gasped and stumbled backward.

My fingers sought out anything they could hold on to and tightened on the edge of the table. His burning gaze was dead set on me as my eyes darted around maniacally, afraid to meet his. Radcliff wasn't hiding anymore—he was letting me see who he was, and that was terrifying.

I gulped before finding the courage to crane my neck. My stare collided with his, and when I did, my terror dissipated.

The light of the candles illuminated half of his face. The half that was perfect and untouched. The other half, the one that was dark and scarred, was hidden in the shadows.

My chin up, I held my breath to not give away my thoughts. He was analyzing me, letting me observe him like a monster in a circus. It was a test. He wanted fear, but I wouldn't give it to him.

I stared at the gruesome slices in his face, as if he had been cut by blades. A long scar traveled from his cheek and cut through the middle of his eyebrow. The part of his skin surrounding the scar was mottled and ridged. The splotchy scar was darker than his skin tone, similar to the thorns of a rose. It looked like he had been burned by hell itself. His scar was old, but it felt like it could reopen at any moment and expose the layer of skin hidden behind the wound.

My gaze froze on his bloodshot left eye, with vessels that had burst inside. Fine filaments tarnished the white of it to plunge into the darkness of his black pupils. A part of me screamed that behind Radcliff's apparent coolness, a boundless hellfire was raging in every one of his cells.

But I didn't feel disgusted by that half of him. On the contrary, it held an entire world of story, a road map to the pain lurking underneath his skin.

What happened to him? What cruelty did that man suffer? What shaped him to be the man he was today? Hundreds of questions spiraled in my mind.

He was human, after all.

The Devil had bled. He had a vulnerability. A human's past. He knew about pain.

"Aren't you scared, little witch?" he muttered, danger in his voice.

"No." I wasn't.

I'd been surrounded by my own demons; he couldn't compete against them. For one reason: I could put a face on him while I was never able to put a face on the ones in the dark.

A hard knot constricted my throat, making it hard to breathe. "What happened?"

"What makes you feel I want to talk about it with you?" The way he pronounced *with you* was as if I was an abomination to him, a curse he couldn't get rid of.

"You're the one who wanted me here," I deadpanned.

"Don't make me regret that decision."

His lips curled into a slight snarl, sending the sensation of a spider crawling down my back. Radcliff was so controlled, almost artificial, to the point that one would wonder if he was capable of feeling anything at all. At the most, right now, I was entertaining him like a puppet you could easily dispose of.

"You're here because I want you to create a perfume for me," he added.

My core awakened. My breath quickened. "W-What?"

"You heard me. And you'll be using the Devil's Corpse."

The flower. My attention sparkled like a shark smelling blood. I was hyperalert.

"Obviously, that perfume will be strictly your creation, and you'll be working on it alone. You'll have until the first day of spring to succeed, and you'll remain in Ravencliff Manor as my guest until then."

I was without a voice.

Was I intrigued? Yes.

Did I want to study that flower and create a masterpiece? Heaven, yes.

Was I seriously considering this? Hell, yes.

He spoke to my obsession, the one that saved me from a life I didn't want but cursed me into an endless torment.

"Why? Why couldn't my uncle—"

"Your uncle is an impostor." He ground out the words between clenched teeth with the authority of a man who was not to be crossed. "His faults, not your own. I'll give you a generous compensation if you're worthy of my time. Needless to say, your uncle will pay a consequential price if you refuse my kind offer."

"What kind of price?" It seemed like a choice, but we both knew I had none. I was a bug trapped inside a spider's web.

He edged closer, his breath near my nape. "You'll make that perfume. Willingly or by force. Unless you prefer I take something else from you." His eyes lingered to my curves before he hit me with a deadly stare.

I folded my arms on my chest. "Why are you doing this?"

"Because I can." His voice hardened ruthlessly. "How do you think you arrived here in the first place?"

A knife-sharp grin twisted his mouth, and the hair on my skin raised on alert. "I was the escort of—" His eyes latched on to me, making me second-guess my next words, "—a friend."

"The one with a stolen invitation."

"How did you—" I stopped midsentence. "You knew I was coming. How? Did you make that happen?"

"Odds." He rolled his tarot card between his fingers with ease.

And then, he made it disappear. "Your *friend* is the one that brought you to me."

"And how did you know he would?"

"If you believe the rumors, I can read anyone's soul. The rest is just gamble, and I never lose."

From the start, it had all been a game. Adonis was the pawn from the moment the invitation was delivered to him. I was the bait. He was the puppet master, orchestrating everything from afar.

"Why did you bother doing all of that?" I swallowed, feeling tingling on my fingers.

"Because, little witch, you've passed my test." His hands gripped the table behind me, his body closing in on mine. The sudden proximity stole my breath. "Which brings us back to the point. The only reason for your presence here."

If he could truly read my soul, he'd know that I would sacrifice everything to revolutionize the world of perfume and to bring to life my dream. He didn't have to bargain with me, only to tempt me with a scent. He could use me, play with me, but I'd do the same. "What perfume are you expecting me to do?"

He thought this through, his dark eyes surveying me with such intensity that it was hard to hold his stare. "Not today."

He swept into the darkness, becoming one with it, his black coat easily interpreted as the Devil's cape. And just like that, I knew he was done with me—for tonight.

The chill running down my spine was a warning.

Welcome to hell, Lily.

Chapter 8

Lily

Dead branches click-clacked on the windows.

The breeze howled like the shrill of a banshee.

The creaky floor filled the dead silence.

I was inside what I should call my bedroom, in which the twilight struggled to penetrate. The space remained dimmed, despite the fact I had pushed the curtains away from the windows and lit up all the lights.

Another clear sign the manor was ruled by a ghost was that I had my phone back. It was placed symmetrically on the center of the bed, a detail that screamed of perfectionism and rigidity. A detail that leaves no place for mistakes.

I rushed to my phone, swallowing down the disappointment when I saw I hadn't received any messages from my uncle. On the other hand, Adonis had filled my notifications with some calls and messages after Radcliff's party.

Adonis: Where are you, Lily?

Adonis: Lily? Can you at least reply?! I'm beginning to worry here.

Adonis: Call me as soon as you get this. Can I come to your place?

I took a shaky breath. I had to call Adonis. At least someone was worried about me, even though he had left without me. It wasn't probably his fault but Radcliff's. I stared upon the balcony. The trees were prison bars with the impossibility to break free from them. The more the darkness thrashed around the bedroom, the more the chills in my core spread.

I brought the phone to my ear, hearing the first beep. I locked my eyes with the spindly fingers of the spooky oak tree. It felt like they wanted to catch me and keep me there. The dying limbs seemed to grow closer, the moonlight shrinking under the force of the obscurity of the sky. Another beep. The nature around the manor was perishing slowly, probably in the image of its owner.

"Lily! Finally! What's happening? Where are you?" Adonis's voice echoed, making me flinch and snap away from my thoughts.

"I'm fine. I—" There was no way to phrase my current situation. "I'm still at Ravencliff Manor. It's a long story."

"What?" he shouted. "You're with him?" The disapproval in his voice hung like a bitter aftertaste. "Did he do something to you?"

"No, he didn't. I'm just his guest." *More or less.*

"When are you coming back?"

My heart locked inside my throat. "I'm not sure yet. I may have an opportunity here. I don't know when—"

"What are you talking about?" His voice raised an octave.

"It's about perfume. You know how much it means to me,"

I blurted out. "I can't tell you more. I've signed a confidentiality agreement."

"You need to get out."

My mouth shut under his warning. The smell of charcoal filled my nostrils as if flames of an old chimney had risen.

"It's not safe, Lily," he continued. "I don't remember what the fuck happened during the party. One minute I was drinking, the next I awoke in the back seat of my car, some strange man in a suit knocking on my window. I was back in front of my house in Paris with a note that said, 'You've broken the rules by stealing an invitation that did not belong to you.' *He* made it happen, Lily." His voice was thick with insinuation.

A chill froze me to the spot, knowing it was just a glimpse of Radcliff's power. I was trapped inside one of the Devil's games, and now I had to protect not only my uncle, but Adonis too.

I couldn't tell him that he was just a pawn, so instead, I hid the truth. "What matters is that you arrived home safely. With all the alcohol you drank, perhaps it was better this way."

"He's dangerous, don't you understand?" he screamed. "I'm picking you up."

"No," I cut him off. "I'm not afraid of him. I know what I'm doing." That was a lie. I was lost, with each of my nerves shrieking inside. But the Devil probably had ears everywhere.

"You can't trust Radcliff. He's a freaking monster! It's disgusting how he's keeping you there. Why would you want to stay, anyway? To play the social climber? Don't be fucking stupid!"

A single drop of grief welled up from the corner of my eye. I stared at nothing, listening to Adonis's outburst of disapproval. The solemn tear fell down my cheek, my body controlled compared to how tangled my mind was. I was stuck between crossroads, burying all those unanswered questions inside it.

"I need to go. I'll keep you updated. Take care," I finally said.

"Lily, I'm sorry, I—"

I hung up the phone and sat on the edge of my bed, a growing void inside me threatening to swallow me whole. Fighting the desire to let myself be carried away by my emotions, I hastened to take my scented candle from my bag.

It had always been a ritual between mom and me. Thanks to it, she was able to rock me to sleep when I was a child. I placed the candle on my dresser before lighting it with a match and letting the scent of ylang-ylang calm my nerves.

Taking back my phone, I ventured across the web, researching the name Radcliff. That's all I knew about him. A name. Was it a last name? A first name? No way to know. The man was even a phantom in the digital age.

My research led to absolutely nothing. Typing "Ravencliff Manor" didn't bring me much success. The results were just a bunch of rumors and scary tales—the ones everyone knew about. Accidentally, I came across some societies owned by Radcliff. *Jewels.* Even there, it wasn't clear what this man was up to.

I gave up. He'd succeeded in the impossible, erasing all traces of him, creating the perfect mystery. The stairs creaked, the sound of footsteps approaching. I glanced at the door, checking it was closed, and once I did, I pulled myself under the blankets of the bed, not feeling safe.

The footsteps stopped at my door. An amber light lit up the hallway. I held my breath, distinguishing the shadow under the doorstep. The air caressed the underside in a shrill noise. My eyes flickered to the handle, begging it not to move. My body tensed in front of all the possibilities. What if Radcliff had come to collect more from me? What if I was truly in danger?

But seconds later, whoever that was dropped a plate of food behind the door and left. I finally exhaled the breath I was holding and turned around to the other side of the bed.

My eyes stuck on the flame of the candle. I waited for the light to fade, for the scent to give off its last final note, before finally drifting myself to sleep.

Dark circles had formed under my eyes due to my lack of sleep. My stomach grumbled; I hadn't eaten anything yesterday. This morning, the plate of food was gone, and I had no other choice but to leave my pretty cage or starve of hunger.

My dress swayed with the draught when I went down the stairs. I followed the smell of pastries that filled the grand ballroom. The sun was hidden by the raven curtains on the huge glass windows. I shuffled forward in the hallway, tightening the sleeves of my robe on my chest.

I drifted cautiously into the dining room area, arriving in front of the old fireplace, where Mrs. Walton was serving breakfast on the regal oak table. She gave me a nod showing me a seat to take.

I did as she silently ordered, the odor of croissants and pains aux chocolats making my stomach rumble across the room.

"Thank you." I smiled coyly as she served me some homemade orange juice.

I thought she'd take a seat alongside me, but she remained like stone. "You don't want to sit?"

She shook her head.

"Will Radcliff join me?" *Please, say no.*

She shook her head again.

"Did you prepare all that for me?"

She nodded and gestured for me to eat, probably tired of my questions. I took a bite of the hot croissant, then another, under the observing stare of Mrs. Walton. I honestly ate like a hungry ogre; it wasn't polite nor classy, but it seemed to please Mrs. Walton as she delivered me a warm smile—unless I was amusing her.

Unfortunately, the stern and cold Radcliff passed behind my back at this exact moment. He left an icy shiver creeping through my spine, and a piece of croissant got stuck in my throat. I coughed and struggled to swallow, cleaning my hands gracefully on the napkin.

Radcliff eyed me just for a slight second before ignoring me with disdain. He was reading a book, the kind that had gilding and a vintage hardcover.

"Good morning," I said in an attempt to have a discussion with at least one human being in this manor.

His gaze slithered over me, up and down, and I felt like the strangest creature he had laid eyes upon. The way he stood regally with a lethal calm was enough to make me lose my composure.

"Lily." My name rolling off his lips sounded like poison.

His scar was menacing, but each of his words was deadly.

When Radcliff was about to leave, I acted on impulse and got up from my chair to stalk toward him. "Are you going to tell me what perfume you want me to create or not? I need a fragrance brief."

His expression was unreadable; it was clear no one would have the ascendancy over a man like him. The least I could do was to defend my position and lift my chin up for what was left of my self-confidence.

"If not, I have nothing else to do here."

He pressed his lips into a thin line as cruel amusement flickered in his eyes. I had awakened something in him, a wicked interest. Even the thorns of his scar seemed to burrow deeper under his skin.

He loomed over me, inching forward with an imposing step that would shake all the stones of the manor. "I'll tell you what to do."

A dull pain arrived in my chest, and I saw him take a threatening form. As he maintained that illusion, I felt small, crushed by his large and imposing shadow. The room was imbued with his presence.

"You'll clean up the fucking mess you've made inside my green-house. I want it spotless. Mr. Walton will give you everything you need." He said it in a diabolical way, as if we were playing a game, in which he was certain to come out the winner. "It should occupy you all day. After all, witches are familiar with brooms."

Irritation should have grown inside me under the coldness of his words. Anger should have thrummed through my veins under the task ordered. But the only emotion that simmered inside me was joy. Radcliff thought he was giving me a punishment, but he gave me a safe haven.

A smile highlighted my face. Returning back to the greenhouse was the only thing I wanted. It brightened my day and dissolved my loneliness.

"I'll clean everything."

His brows slanted inward, betraying it wasn't the answer he was expecting.

"And I'm sorry. For the mess," I added.

His throat bobbed, his obsidian eyes firmly set on mine for an instant. They had a shade of purple, just like a black tulip blooming in the dead of the night.

Radcliff disappeared through the dim hallway. He and the ob-scure nestled like old friends, his departure allowing the light to shine brighter.

It was only when I entered the greenhouse with Mr. Walton that I realized the mess I had made. My heart shattered upon facing the disaster. My fear of being trapped in the dark had brought chaos to what I cherished the most. I was guilty.

"It's all my fault," I whispered, out of breath.

It was a battlefield, with wilting plants and broken pots. My eyes swiveled to every corner. Potting soil was spilled on the ground, accompanied by dead flowers that had been trampled—a storm would have caused as much damage. I pulled myself together, taking a deep breath.

"I'll need a bucket of soapy water," I instructed Mr. Walton, who took some notes next to me.

I dropped my jacket on the handle. Tied up my hair in a ponytail. Inhaled the scent of the Devil's Corpse. I had been so captivated and obsessed by this plant that I had ignored the other damaged flowers until now.

A thick cloud of smoke escaped my lips. I was convinced I could make the flowers reborn by springtime. I hastened to the tool shed and grabbed a broom. Moss and algae had started colonizing the greenhouse in a green color. I turned around to Mr. Walton, the tune of my voice higher. "Alongside a homemade vinegar spray, please."

He bowed his head and left. The greenhouse lacked care; saving it would take me more work than I thought. As I removed all the pots from the greenhouse to the courtyard, the breeze ran through the trees and rippled to my bones in a chill.

I carried the new potting soil, struggling to hold the heavy bags, my gaze momentarily set on the sparkling clear water of the fountain in the center of the courtyard. It was almost transparent and frosted due to the wintry weather.

Mr. Walton startled me by arriving with the cleaning bucket. I let the bags crash onto the ground, dispersing the soil at my feet. *Great.* He gave me a perplexed expression, slightly raising an eyebrow. The kind that meant, "You're taking too many liberties. Radcliff won't like it."

I smiled nonetheless, proving to the old man that I shouldn't be underestimated. "Thank you."

I continued my extravaganza. With all the exotic plants outside—apart from the Devil's Corpse —I attacked the scrubbing and rinsing. I made each surface sparkle, not minding getting covered in dirt and for some strands of my hair to dampen from the sweat on my forehead.

Mr. Walton kept an eye on me, probably at the orders of Radcliff. He supervised me from his bench in the garden, his eyes popping over the top of his newspaper from time to time.

The greenhouse was my sanctuary.

The flowers were my friends. Each of their roots, petals, and green leaves spoke to me.

After the cleaning, I glued the pieces of broken pots together before offering them a new beginning. Gardening was the metaphor of life. It taught me we reap what we sow, to have patience and, most importantly, faith. Faith it'd grow, no matter the damage the plants had lived.

No one had taken care of that greenhouse. They'd survived only with a little care. The strict minimum. They weren't understood. Their exposition, temperatures, and care provided were all wrong. The varied colors of blossoms, the lipstick-pink peonies to the hibiscus, orchids, Amazon lilies, and pansies, could have formed the most enchanting sunset of colors. But they had been left to die, their petals tarnished.

"Do you have bigger pots?" I raised my voice at Mr. Walton, focused on the task at hand, my hands protected by gloves plunging into the soil.

He cleared his throat and walked away.

The orchids had been drowned inside the water. Their roots were dead. They needed freedom, yet they were imprisoned inside their small plots. I cut off the dead buds and left the roots behind for the orchid to hold to something inside the new pot they'd have.

"Here you go. You're free." I gazed hopefully at the flowers, thrilled to have given them a new life.

Mr. Walton eventually came back with bigger pots, then

returned to reading another newspaper. In a trance with my task, I had thrown dirt all over my face and my clothes. I'd made the greenhouse into a construction site.

Finally done with repotting the flowers, I took sight of Mrs. Walton coming to join us with refreshments. She sat alongside her husband, both of them locking eyes with mine, their heads bowing to one side. They probably wondered what the hell I was doing.

"I'm almost done!" I waved at the couple, mid-laugh and halfway out of breath when I carried the flowers back to the greenhouse.

They remained silent and stoic, observing me as an inhuman creature. I readjusted and changed the arrangement of the flowers inside the greenhouse, pushing the pots like an American football player during a melee. The sun had turned around the glass roof of the dome, going from a golden white to a purple sunset.

My back ached, and I struggled to stand on my legs. Every part of my body hurt. I was dirty and probably covered in plants, judging by the strong earthy odor. I was finally done. The Waltons were gone; it was just me and the flora. The greenhouse was now a royal court, the Devil's Corpse for the queen, her thorns for guards, the other flowers for subjects. The carnage had passed, and everything looked shiny and sparkling. Warm and inviting. *Hopeful.*

Proud to have accomplished the impossible, I strolled in the direction of the manor. I was determined to find Radcliff and to slap my victory in his face despite my exhaustion. The manor was ghostly silent as I paced the grand ballroom, my feet tapping a quick rhythm against the floor.

I let out a shallow exhale, my eyes flashing to Radcliff enthroned regally on an armchair. He was reading through the same book by the fireplace. My steps echoed on the floor in his direction, but he didn't shoot me one glance. Instead, he turned a page, not acknowledging my presence.

I removed my gardening gloves and threw them on the pages, leaving him no choice. He lifted his eyes, blazing me with hellfire. He slammed his book, a muscle in his jaw clenching. His hard stare lingered on my dirty clothes, my sweaty hair, and the roots of plants stuck on them.

"Your greenhouse is spotless." With the palm of my hand, I swiped some potting soil off my forehead, feeling uncomfortable. My heart hammered like a scared animal, every fiber of my body wanting to flee. "I took the liberty of rearranging some things. Your flowers were dying and lacking care. By spring, it should flourish beautifully."

He fell backward on his seat, one of his fingers passing through his plush lips. His chest rumbled low as he spoke. "You've spent all day on it."

"Yes."

A silence fell between us, the kind that raised the hair on my arms.

"I didn't mind doing it," I added in a whisper, as if I was treading water, searching for my breath.

He lifted himself from his seat, and my nostrils flared. He smelled of nightmares and fantastical dreams. A mystical land on a rainy day under the moonlight. A dark symphony melting with the lava of a volcano.

"You asked what perfume I want you to create for me." He passed in front of me and stopped.

The silk fabric of his suit brushed my arm. We were side by side, our bodies aligned, yet they were shifted in the opposite direction.

"Yes." I gulped.

"I'll show you."

Necks turned, but bodies frozen, the dark mirth in his gaze swiveled to my brown eyes.

"We're going to my... club." A sardonic hint of a smile drew across his face. "But I'll not be responsible for you, and I ask for you to be discreet. Don't make a show of yourself. I won't be your savior or anything—you're on your own."

Just like I had been all of my life.

I folded my arms over my chest. "I can take care of myself."

"You've seen nothing yet." His words, like venom, caressed my nape. "I suggest you change. You have ten minutes."

Chapter 9

Lily

The alley of Club 7 was deserted, similar to one of those scary scenes where murders happen. The imposing metallic back door of the club was guarded by three men with strong figures, as if whatever was inside would never see the light of the day. The bouncers bowed in front of Radcliff and slid the door open.

All I needed was one step inside to be transported to another universe. The lights and the rich wallpaper were a burning red. The sensual music gave me goose bumps. The servers were dressed in elegant costumes, serving all types of aphrodisiacs and exotic food. It was over-the-top splendor with big stained glass, corrupting their holy meaning, the air charged with debauchery and secrets.

In the main area, some intimate and private spaces with velvet couches were displayed. They were occupied mostly by men in expensive suits with a substantial wallet size. Politicians. Businessmen.

Men with a shady reputation. They were all here, tasting Radcliff's possessions, their evil laughter vibrating into my whole core.

At the bar, alcohol and cash flew without pause. But what surprised me most was the show. A mix of the beauty of a Parisian cabaret with the exhilaration of a circus and the vice of a gentleman's club. It felt like we'd jumped into the craziness of the roaring twenties.

On the stage, under the spotlight, there was a girl with a square pink wig who was executing an aerial dance. She was naked with only glitter covering her intimate parts. She was sensual, the reincarnation of every man's desires. All eyes were on her before a couple of other girls joined her for a glamorous performance. They were goddesses, Aphrodites, sirens, weakening men's souls. There was something addicting about this show. A certain freedom to be who you wanted for an instant.

I didn't agree with any of this. I didn't belong here. That splendor disguise was a lie; it smelled fake. Radcliff had tricked the sight of his guests into making them believe it was the Eurasian field, but he couldn't trick my nose. The only thing missing in this sumptuous debauchery was the intoxicating scent.

That's when I understood Club 7 was a depiction of each sin.

Greed.

Gluttony.

Lust.

Wrath.

Pride.

Sloth.

Envy.

"Radcliff."

I turned around, hearing the voice of a woman. To my surprise, she was the one who'd mocked me before the hunt on New Year's Eve. Her luscious dress displayed each of her perfect curves, her red lipstick beautifying her femme fatale look with glossy raven hair.

There was no need to pretend she did not know how appealing her look was, and she was using it. Radcliff remained silent alongside me while she glared in my direction.

"I recognize you." She inspected me from head to toe, a frozen smile on her face.

I wrinkled my nose at the smell of her. Her fresh green notes, a mix of galbanum and mint, itched my nostrils in a burning sensation.

"Melissa. Lily," Radcliff finally spoke, but he couldn't be more bored to present us. "I have some business to attempt."

"Don't worry, I'll babysit her," she offered, placing her long manicured black nails on Radcliff's bicep possessively.

The lethal calm of Radcliff's licorice eyes met mine. He smoothed his tie, forcing Melissa to retract her hand. Silence washed over us, Radcliff probably considering her offer. The intensity of his stare was impossible to hold on to, and I drifted my eyes to the ground.

Radcliff took his leave without speaking a word and headed to the top floor. I lifted my face heavenward, scrutinizing the enormous glass window upstairs. It gave a 180-degree view of the club.

"That's Radcliff's office. Don't get any ideas. It's strictly forbidden," Melissa commented.

"That's why we can't see anything through it." I was fascinated to discover what could be behind those windows.

Melissa snickered. "Are you surprised?"

I shook my head, keeping my gaze on it. The private one-way window offered the ability to be invisible while seeing everything that was happening down here.

Radcliff was undeniably the king of the underworld.

"So… You're staying at Ravencliff Manor." Melissa took a seat in the bar area and asked, "What are you doing there?"

"I'm here to make perfume."

Her eyes opened wildly before she exploded with laughter. I tensed, slightly offended about her finding me that amusing.

When she realized I wasn't joking, she focused her attention on the barman. She leaned in, drawing a seductive smile while showing him a perfect view of the valley between her breasts. "Something strong. That would make me good, Paulo." She then gave me an interrogative eyebrow. "You?"

"Nothing for me. I don't drink." By the way her eyebrows furrowed, I knew I was the definition of boring to her. I sat next to her, asking the first question that came to mind. "Radcliff and you are a thing?"

"Once upon a time." She bit the cherry of her martini with a devious smile. "We were each other's first, and that's something you never forget. Am I right?"

She dared me.

She wanted to know.

To have the upper hand.

"Right," I had to reply, hiding my discomfort. I wasn't one to share my past, especially the intimate one with a stranger.

"Ladies." I was saved by the bell when the rasp of a man's voice echoed next to us.

We turned our heads in synchronization toward the stranger.

Black pepper and cinnamon.

The spiciness of his scent couldn't be ignored—unique but still unpleasant to me. The realization of who the stranger was twisted my stomach.

Adonis's father. Christian Carmin.

In his early fifties, he was probably one of the most influential people in France. His face was on every billboard. He had the kind of Mediterranean tan you only got on a yacht during this season. A tailored suit that screamed of every shade of money and power and the same piercing blue eyes as his son.

"I've never had the pleasure to see you here. But you seem familiar," Christian addressed me with the confidence of a man who is used to getting what he wants. With his pristine white grin, everyone knew he was a charming talker.

We'd actually met once. I went rigid at the memory of it, as if a corrosive liquid gnawed at my insides. He didn't even recognize me.

"She's Radcliff's protégée," Melissa said, sweeping her hand with disinterest. "Lily something."

Christian quipped back, "I wasn't asking you, Melissa."

I swiveled my eyes to Radcliff's office. A part of me could feel his presence behind the glass. My stare remained stuck on it with the belief he would hear my silent inner scream, like someone who held on to a rope with the fear of falling. But the tingling in my eyes made me come back to Melissa and Christian.

His gaze was firmly set on me, ignoring Melissa's gunning eyes. With sparkling interest, Christian continued. "You have the face of a model. Maybe it is where I know you from? Which agency are you from?"

"I'm not a model." I smiled politely, ignoring the hair rising on my skin. "I'm friends with your son, Adonis."

A vivid glow lit up his eyes alongside a beam. "Oh, right." He stroked my arm like we were relatives, a feeling of discomfort lashing across my stomach. He held a smile on his face before he added, "Lily Bellerose. My son is very fond of you."

"I'm—I—" I stammered, not knowing what to say.

"Well, if you need anything, princess, I'll be your man. If you're interested in a change of career, I have some contacts in the modeling world." He handed me his card. "And Adonis's girlfriends are always welcome to the house."

I struggled to swallow a knot in my throat. The first and last time I went to Adonis's place, I didn't feel at ease. I always had a bad, unfounded feeling about Christian. I'd probably misunderstood the situation back then. He had been nice to me. Too nice. Too friendly.

I never talked about it with Adonis; it was his father, after all. But the way he touched my inner thigh that day hadn't been innocent. The way his hand traveled to places he shouldn't—

"Mr. Carmin, maybe you'd like to head to your table?" Hugo saved me by delicately placing one of his hands behind my back, interrupting us. No doubt that Hugo was imposing, but in a gentle way. The contrary of Radcliff. "Lily, Radcliff is waiting for you in his office."

"You deserve a promotion, Hugo," Christian said in a patronizing kind of way, before posing his hand on Hugo's shoulder.

Melissa leaned in toward me. "Men. They are all the same— they don't keep their interest long," she hinted quietly with malice. "One minute you're the queen of their eyes, the next one, they toss you away. Terrifying, isn't it?"

Christian shot a last glance at me as he and Hugo were about to leave. "Lily, would you join me?"

No. I didn't want to. All eyes were on me. The flaming ones of Melissa. The hurry-the-fuck-up stare of Hugo. The sparkling ones of Christian. My heart jumped in my throat, a feeling of strangulation, as if a cord encircled my neck, suffocating me.

"I'm sorry, I can't. Radcliff is waiting for me. I should go." I got up from my seat, ready to finally see what was behind the glass window. "It was nice to meet you again, Mr. Carmin."

"Surely Mr. Radcliff can wait." Christian's hand reached for mine. I was screaming inside when his thumb brushed mine. "It'd be a pleasure to talk about my son with you, please."

I dug my nails inside my palm.

"S-Sure."

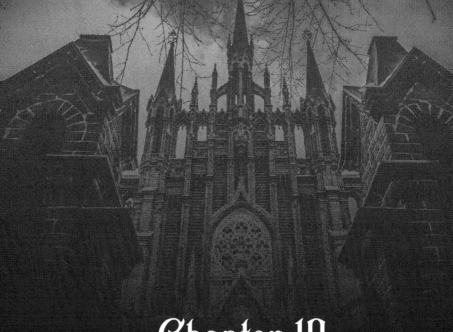

Chapter 10

Radcliff

"Thank you, Mr. Radcliff," LeBon said weakly with shaking hands.

He probably hadn't slept for days. For an incorruptible judge with a rare sense of right and wrong and a true example of justice, he had no sense of presentation, not bothering to adjust his suit properly. He wasn't old, in his forties, and yet he had gained at least ten years today. The bastard had made it his personal goal to be part of my downfall, and his dearest wish was to bring me to trial. And now, here he was inside my club's office.

"Make this quick." I was already bored.

"Sure, sure, I…" He trailed off. "I need your help." *Shocking.* "I want personal revenge on an untouchable man. I know you can introduce me to some people… You have contacts, and I was hoping—"

"I said quick."

"Christian Carmin, he—" He struggled to articulate. "He violated my eighteen-year-old daughter. And not just once. You have to help me. She's stuck on an internship with Carmin to study fashion. It's her biggest dream and… He did so many—"

And here were the crocodile tears.

He stopped talking to let his gut-wrenching sobs tear through his chest. Another human would be touched by this display of weakness. I wasn't. Yeah, Carmin was a disgusting jerk who abused women, most of them young and in search of stardom. Everyone knew it—except for his foolish, blind son—but nobody had proof. We had a fake politeness. Business was business, after all, and I wasn't known to have any principles.

In any other way, not my problem.

"Why do you think I'd be interested in making an agreement with you." It wasn't a question. I wasn't interested. Heroes fight for good causes: they "help" people. Villains fight for gains.

"Didn't you just hear what he did to—"

"If you're looking for someone who cares, you came to the wrong person. I can't help you, nor do I have the desire to."

I nodded to the security guards, signaling them to take him away.

"Wait. I'll give you everything I have. I'm a judge—I'll work for you. I'll do anything. That's how it works, right? My soul for your help. That's why they call you the Devil…"

A sardonic smile drew over my lips. "Beg."

"S-Sorry?" he stuttered.

"Beg," I gritted out between clenched teeth.

He swallowed his pride, facing the truth. I would humiliate him and his ego enough that it'd haunt him to his grave. It was his admission fee for wanting to go against me in the past.

"Please, I'm begging you. She's everything I have."

"Beg harder." I loomed over him, unmoved by his weakness.

He curved his trembling body in a submissive way. Then, he bowed down, falling on his knees. "I beg you."

Those words ripped him apart.

As for me, I had to admit it, having one more judge under my ruling was always a safe bet. Especially this desperate one. Once again, human weakness. LeBon was a good man but a stupid one.

Contrary to what people thought, I didn't take pleasure in all of this. I had no feelings, good or bad. I was a peaceful man as long as people respected my rules, didn't try to cross me, or cheat with the contract.

"Pick a card," I ordered, displaying the set of tarot cards in front of him.

LeBon, to my surprise, did as asked without a word. He rose up hesitantly and pointed at a card, staring at me with wide eyes. I turned the card around only to notice it was ironically *The Justice*. Just like I thought—good man but stupid principles.

"You know it's true." He peered at the card, conflict rising inside of him. "I would have never come to a man like you. I despise all of you. But despite who I am, my hands are tied. I want him to pay, and protect my daughter. I hope you'll use your power to do something right, Mr. Radcliff. Please."

His eyes betrayed his disgust and hatred for me, but his soul was powerless. A lost one.

"You'll receive a contract tomorrow that I'm expecting back within twenty-four hours, or you'll pay the price. Your daughter will receive a full scholarship abroad at Malarin School of Fashion, which if I recall is the best in the world. She'll follow it with, of course, an internship with the most talented creators of the century. However, I don't do personal revenge." I was smart enough not to create unnecessary drama in business.

I stuck my stare on LeBon, whose eyes had tripled in size.

"Congratulations, Mr. LeBon, your daughter's future will be bright. Yours, on the contrary…"

With one sharp gesture from me, the guards took him away. I lit up a cigar, the pungent smoke twirling skyward. So many people chased after the light; they forgot we were born and would die in the darkness. It was only there we were our true selves.

Look at them. My lips turned cruel around the corners as I observed through the security cameras the guests fucking inside the red dungeons and practicing BDSM. The crowd inside my club wasn't better. Each of their gestures and laughter hid the void of their pitiful existence.

All of my money came from investments. Jewel businesses and diamond mines. Everything was legal, which was one of the reasons most people hated and envied me. One, I had power. Two, they couldn't blackmail me since I had no feelings whatsoever. Three, I was untouchable and technically doing nothing wrong. I made my own kingdom with its justice and rules.

A thick cloud of silver-blue smoke, like the hottest of fires, obscured the office in the sweetest of blurs. I didn't take any side, good or bad, which was why people came to me. I was able to deliver them the privacy they needed. Mafia bosses would meet to discuss alliances as powerful men would be free to expose their desires.

I exchanged favors for a piece of their soul. Most of the time I was an intermediary, introducing people together through this club. Sometimes, I'd even help with their money problem or be the solution to a situation they wanted to escape. I knew everyone's most somber secrets here. I even threw exuberant parties to create the perfect image. I was the invisible man in the dark, who delivered the pleasures they sought and favors they craved.

My eyes roamed across the club, locking on something rather unpleasant. My edge of irritation had returned at the sight of Lily discussing with Carmin, and his repulsive persona hidden behind his Ken's artificial smile. She hadn't done as she was asked. She was making me wait after I requested her up here.

"What does she think she's doing," I growled.

Melissa was doing what she usually did, flirting with people and being the center of attention. She was the closest thing to a friend, I guess. We understood each other, but I was sick of her attention seeking. As for Hugo, he stood like a fucking statue. Did anyone follow orders around here?

Anger rose in me like a tide. Carmin was leering over Lily. Everyone could see it except her. She was too naive for her own good. Beauty was the weakness of every man here, so of course they ogled Lily. I didn't need to be a mind reader to guess their thoughts.

She was a breath of fresh air in this perversion, an angel at the mercy of demons.

I didn't like it.

Not one bit.

She wasn't mine. But that didn't mean she could be someone else's.

I was here to do business, and here I was babysitting a child. I cursed the Devil's Corpse, regretting my impulsive choice of having her at Ravencliff Manor. I loathed the fact I wasn't indifferent to her. How innocent her smile was. And most importantly, the way she'd corrupted Cerba. That dog liked no one, apart from me and Hugo, and in less than one day, they became best friends.

Her beauty hardened my cock. Her strange behavior had made me watch her all day through the cameras like a perv. Cleaning the greenhouse was a punishment for disturbing my peace. Yet, it felt like I'd offered her an amusement park. That devotion and passion of hers captivated me.

She created unwanted thoughts that crept through my mind.

I wanted to kill her hope.

That was what I despised the most about her. The hope she was cursing me with.

"Why did you even bring her here?" Hugo had asked earlier.

"I need to see if she's up for the task. I don't like wasting my time," I had replied. Little did I know, I'd be wasting my time at this precise moment.

I stubbed my cigar on the ashtray, my eyes narrowing at Lily. I smoothed my tie, dark thoughts of how I'd teach her a lesson for messing with my patience slithering through my veins, slow but searing, like the deadliest of the scourge.

I stormed out of my office. Time was valuable. I was a busy man. Each second, I made hundreds of dollars. Each second, another person heard about how much of a monster I was. Each second, I was giving right to their gossip.

Cursing internally, I shut down the fucking electricity before passing through the crowd like a phantom. My eyes stuck on Lily, and fury ran red through my brain. I had one mission. I walked faster, ignoring the gasps of the crowd and their loud noises.

Arriving next to them, I muttered to Hugo, "Put the goddamn power on."

I snatched Lily by her waist, forcing her to come with me. With a firm grip, I held her while pushing the crowd to make our way out. That witch was making it hard for me, moving frenetically. I shut her up with my hand, having no desire to make a spectacle of myself.

"Stay calm." I gritted my teeth.

She stopped her madness but dug her nails into the bare skin of my hand. She could draw blood out of me; it wouldn't stop me from what was coming next. As soon as I slammed the door to my office, I pinned her against it to trap her. The anger pouring through me couldn't be stopped.

Hugo switched the light on at the perfect time.

"When I ask something, I expect you to follow it!" I roared, pounding the door with my fist close to her head.

When I finally looked upon her, she struck me with a mask of panic on her face. A flood of sobs shimmered in her eyes before they gushed down on her ashen cheeks. Her lips shook. Her pupils flared. A muscle in my jaw twitched—I didn't think my grip was that strong. Had I hurt her?

"What—"

In less than a second, arms were wrapped around me.

Body quivering alongside me.

Streams of tears flowed faster than an angry river on my suit.

Her crashing on my chest made me flinch. She tightened her hold on me with all her strength. The perfume of her hair, sweet and addictive, bewitched me. She broke down, merging me with her chaos, sharing with me a glimpse of the pain she was carrying inside of her.

My anger for her vanished. I cursed myself for what I was about to do. I should have pushed her away. Let her deal with her issue. I shouldn't have been put into that position. It wasn't my role. Worse than allowing this, I held her in my arms, reinforcing and hardening the link she created between us.

"What made you cry?" *You, idiot.*

"The light switched off," she whimpered, taking shaky breaths to calm herself down. "It brought back bad memories. I'm better now, but I see things... in the complete dark." She struggled to articulate, her chin shaking as if hunted by an evil she couldn't face.

The greenhouse. It all made sense now. How ironic that the only woman I paid interest to was terrified of the monsters she could not see. She was terrified of everything I represented. Monstrosity and darkness. She was braver than she thought.

"I'm sorry." She held my stare with red, swollen eyes. "For making you mad."

"You should sit." I hid the way she almost destabilized me with her apology by clearing my throat.

She took a seat on my black leather sofa, and I served her a glass of water. I squared an ankle over my knee, sitting in front of her. I contemplated her drinking every last bit of her drink. A part of me would have told her she was safe, but she couldn't count on someone like me.

I was grotesque, a sphinx, half creature, half human, whose ability to care for anyone had been eradicated. But most importantly, I was selfish. If I started wanting her, she'd be mine. And then, no one could protect her from me.

I wasn't a predator.

No, I was all monster.

The one the hero conquered on his quest.

The banished one.

A beast who existed only for a cold purpose.

"What's this place anyway?" She sniffed, erasing one of her tears with her palm, done with her thirst. "What type of man are you?"

The kind who collects souls to his dark realm. "I create a holy garden, an emerald field, while I corrupt each apple for Adam and Eve to fall." I was the snake, the voice saying out loud what they secretly craved. I created a garden, but I would never taste the poisoned apple and fall like they did.

"Will you hurt me?" She tried to read into my soul, having more faith in humans than she should have.

"No." *Not if you keep your distance from me. Not if you disappear from my mind. Not if you stop surprising me.* "But I could." And a part of me wanted to.

I wanted her to be mine.

Mine to play with, possess, and own.

She'd awakened a possessiveness in me I'd never had.

For once, I wanted to taste the apple, and that was dangerous.

"Radcliff…" My body jolted with electricity at the sound of my name on her pouty lips, which were asking to be sucked, beaten, abused. "Which perfume do you want me to create?"

The pulse in her throat betrayed that she already knew the answer to that after what she'd witnessed tonight.

"I think you know, and you smelled it."

The arousal.

The carnal desire.

The fire burning your core.

"An aphrodisiac," she dropped, out of breath.

I ambled through my office, passing behind the sofa, my steps filling the silence. Inside the Devil's Corpse, a powerful aphrodisiac was hidden, multiplying the senses and exposing the most hidden desires. It wasn't the first in history—pumpkin pie, chocolate, maca, ginseng, jasmine, they all were to some degree an aphrodisiac. Throughout time, Roman kings and queens created Spanish fly potions to get what they wanted from their lovers, organizing orgies. Moral of the story? Just like the Marquis de Sade and his whores: dead. All the civilizations tried to achieve it. Not everyone could play the Devil's work. But the Devil's Corpse had a power I'd never encountered before. I had the show, the food, the music—all I was missing was the smell. The aphrodisiac.

I stooped behind Lily, my lips so close to her neck. Her gaze remained stuck on the windows, but the goose bumps on her skin felt my presence.

"Yes," I whispered. I wanted people to show themselves for who they truly were. Weak, pathetic, and easily dominated by their compulsions—while making a good deal of money out of it. And what was better to create the most exquisite torture on Earth, to submit to your desires that weaken you, than an angel herself.

"It's impossible," she stated.

"Well, you better make it possible, then, Lily. Because if you don't…" My hand skimmed across the bare skin on her shoulder. "Let's hope you do."

She whirled around, standing up from the couch. Facing me, she pierced me with flames of hatred in her eyes. It was almost cute.

"You're a monster." *Finally.*

"Don't act so surprised, little witch."

"You're crazy." She spat out the words as if she were reciting an incantation, casting a curse on me.

A sneer drew across my lips. "I'll take it as a compliment."

Her lower lip quivered. I thought she'd rush away in fear, but she maintained eye contact despite her watery eyes. "I want to be able to make my own perfume. That's my condition."

"What gave you the impression we were negotiating here?" There was no way out for her—she knew it.

"I'll do your science fiction demand." *Of course you will.* "But I want to be able to make a side perfume for myself using that plant. Favor for favor. I don't want any money."

Interesting. She would sell her soul to darkness at the price of her destructive obsession. It amused me. That flower goddess was crazier than she thought. She was just too blind to see it.

"Give me a reason."

"Because I'm the only one who can do this." Her eyes were dead set on me. "That's why you chose me. Because you know I'll sacrifice everything to make it happen. Our goals are linked, despite the fact yours are—" She stopped, biting her next words. Wise decision. "Anyway, deals are never one-sided." She gulped. "You can threaten to kill me. I don't care."

"Now, why would I do that?" A wicked grin twisted my mouth as she seemed to hold her breath in angst. "Lily Bellerose, I believe you just made a deal with the Devil." After all, the sins of her uncle weren't her own. "Now, a car will drive you back."

She raised her chin up, and on her way to leave, she leered at me one last time. Her whole face lit up. "Thank you."

Why was she thanking me? A line appeared between my brows as I watched her sway through the light of the stairs.

I called Hugo, walking again to my glass windows. I started a countdown in my head until Lily appeared. She passed among the crowd, this time following my orders.

"Yeah?" Hugo picked up, the moaning of women echoing through the phone.

Lily shot a last glance in my direction, as if she could feel my presence upstairs. My body was stiff, believing for a moment her eyes could penetrate my invisibility.

"Tear the curtains down in Lily's room, and make sure there are lights in the manor."

"Let the light enter—really?" Hugo joked. "What the fuck happened to you, Rad?"

She happened.

Chapter 11

Lily

I didn't sleep much last night. It wasn't because the manor was deathly cold, nor because of the intermittent creaks or the howling wind tapping on the windows, but the confusion that was clouding my thoughts.

My curtains were removed from my bedroom, a permanent dim light delicately added to it. Yet, when Radcliff wasn't terrorizing me, with his sharp shadows roaming around every room, he was avoiding me like the plague. Unable to resolve the gloomy mystery that he was and the mixed signals he was sending me, I devoted my time to my obsession.

Accompanied by the sounds of screaming breaching the void, I had concocted my own recipe by writing the list of oils I'd need to create the fragrance, my wished-for sources and some possible perfume formulas. I didn't want to belong to the category of the damned and the forgotten.

I wanted to belong to the category of the gifted.

The mad scientist. The genius villain. The haunted musician. No matter what they did and who they were, good or evil, they all had something in common—undeniable talent. Something stronger than mankind, who pushed them toward the road of exception. And today was my chance to be one of them.

At the lab, I felt like an alchemist inside an apothecary lab, where each vial was like philtres, enclosing an odor of magic and love. I was inspecting the oils carefully selected by Radcliff's trader, Patrick Delange—a man who had fifty years of experience in perfume. He had worked during his youth as a nose in France with the biggest perfume houses. My uncle told me they once worked on a project together forever ago. He made a career mostly in dealing with oils, being known for his excellence in matters of quality.

"Are they coming from Grasse?" I asked while opening the flask to soak my strips to smell the oil of rose centifolia.

"Yes. It's last year's batch from the end of May," he replied.

Skeptical, I inhaled the scent. By the end of May, the sun has been burning, inflicting the loss of the sweetness of the rose. I furrowed my brows. The scent was strong but not as captivating and addictive as it should have been. It missed the rich, charming, sugary odor to transport me to some magical land with a candy house and rainbow sky, or a rose-tinted movie with happy endings. It just wasn't the one.

"I'd like to try a batch from the beginning of May."

His lips curled into a placid smile, his eyes unexpressive. "I assure you, this oil is perfectly acceptable. I've never had any complaints from great noses before."

His brownish gaze slithered the length of my body, one of his eyebrows raising slightly under his thin glasses.

I squared my shoulders, a broad smile on my face, determined to not let myself be intimidated. "That's not the one I want." I was the client, after all.

His snort dissolved into a mocking laughter, his head jerking back. "How old are you? Eighteen?"

My mouth opened in an attempt to make him change his mind about me, but he didn't have any desire to hear me out, only to shut me up.

"You don't have any experience in the art of perfume. You're just lucky to be here because you're pre—" he enunciated with bitterness, swallowing the last word, regaining control of himself.

Just because I'm pretty... I took a shaky breath, my hand squeezing the wooden desk behind me. It all rushed back to my mind. The smell of rotten plums and anise in the dormitories, where I read through my genius mother's notes with the hope to connect with her. The thyme and frankincense scent of Mother Anne, making me feel like an impostor who wasn't good enough, crying in the cold cell. All those spicy scents where I thought of shutting down the unstoppable fire burning inside me.

I'd finally learned courage wasn't something you were born with. It was something you learned to be.

I wasn't here because I was pretty.

I was here because I was cursed with something devastating and stronger than I. A promise of a better life. A dream of greatness. A destiny to achieve.

I gulped down my feelings and ignored my shaking hands, as well as my insecurities, slamming inside of me. *Trust yourself. No one else ever will.* I ambled toward the oils, feeling Patrick's gaze glaring at me. I took sight of each flacon, my eyes stopping at the one holding jasmine oil. A nerve twitched inside of me as I discovered its provenance. It was from a big corrupt company interested only in massive moneymaking. I always preferred small and pure companies of quality. They felt like hidden treasures to me.

Which explained why I wasn't satisfied with any of these scents. I wanted my fragrance to create a history. To incarnate love. To transport me somewhere enchanting. Pleasurable. And for that, I needed the most exquisite ingredients of all. The best and the rarest in the market to bring to life the most heady of potions.

"Could you please find me other batches? I have a list." I handed him the list.

He took it with annoyance, readjusting his pine-green turtleneck. "Oh là là…" he huffed while reading. "Let me give you some advice, young lady." Arms crossed on his chest, he narrowed his eyes at me from behind his intellectual glasses. "Stop thinking you'll be the next great nose. You're insignificant, just like everyone. You can't compensate for your lack of talent with pretensions!" He shook the list in his hand and ripped it in one straight move.

I contemplated the pieces of paper falling to the floor, the hope to be taken seriously vanishing in a slow-motion moment. My head bent to the side, the cold shiver behind my back freezing me to stone. From an exterior point of view, I was calm and placid. Even the tear wetting the corner of my eye was silent. From the inside, I was decomposing. Breaking. Ripping.

I clamped my fingers into the flesh of my palm until the pain reached me. Until the scarlet-red color of my blood became a reminder of my anger holding me captive.

Ignore it.

Put it in the box inside of your head.

Don't think of it.

Deny your emotions.

I kept repeating the mantra like an incantation that saved me for so many years.

Patrick wrinkled his nose, an expression of disgust on his face.

"It smells like rotten crap here," he complained, probably referring to the Devil's Corpse odor.

I had spent the first hour of my waking up with this flower, studying it and familiarizing myself with it. I believed we had made a connection. Her odor was probably still on me. Point is, he wasn't smelling the potential power of the Devil's Corpse, just like he doubted my flair. He lacked respect for both of us.

There is no light without darkness. Those were my mother's words, helping me fight back my shadows. I focused, peeling my eyelids closed. I inhaled and smelled our surroundings. I caught the odor of a smoky, tarred scent and burnt wood. I peeled my eyelids open.

"You're right." I faked a smile. "Your perfume doesn't match the pH of your skin." You can't lie with scents. He wanted to show he was an intellectual spending his time in the dust of knowledge, while it made him look like an old book you want to run away from. "You should try some fruity scent. Bergamot, for instance. You know, something sparkly and fresh that would not make you smell like a rotten Maccabee."

Patrick stumbled backward before flashing me a dubious look. We both knew I was right. He secretly craved youth and to be in the spotlight.

He didn't have the time to think of a comeback before Cerba barked at him. She stood like a fearless protector between the devastating tornado that was creeping inside of me and Patrick. He scowled at her, and in response, she showed her canines aggressively.

Patrick slammed the door open, looking back at me. "Trust me when I say you don't have the talent for it."

He stormed away, and I released the breath I was holding. I fell onto my chair. I didn't know what came over me. For an instant, I regretted hurting Patrick with my words. It was as if the thorns of a growing wild plant pierced me from the inside, tearing me apart in a screaming howl. My anger faded, and the thorns retracted, leaving me with a blossoming void inside of me.

I took my phone, hoping to hear some news from my uncle. But he was silent. A silence that could be easily interpreted in so many ways. Adonis, on the contrary, occupied all of my notifications with his messages.

Adonis: Please, come back. It's not safe. You're making a mistake. You can't get involved with a man like Radcliff.

Adonis: Lily, I'm worried.

Cerba lay on my feet, her puppy eyes locking onto me. The warmth of her company comforted me and gave me enough strength to reply to Adonis.

Me: Please, don't worry about me… I know what I'm doing. I need your support, Adonis.

Adonis: I can't support this, Lily...

A cold shiver skittered across my back.

Adonis: What do you want from him?

I felt my thumping heart dropping, knowing he wouldn't understand.

Adonis: Let me know when you're coming back to reason and I'll pick you up.

I left Adonis on seen.

I thought of turning off my phone, but I had faith I could perhaps reach my uncle. The beeps of his phone rang until I was left on his voicemail. Again.

"Hi, Uncle. It's Lily. I wanted to let you know I'm…" *Miserable.* "Fine. You'll see. I'll make that perfume—you don't have to worry. I hope life isn't too hard for you alone in Paris. I miss you. Please, call me back."

I hung up, taking my coat. I shot a glance at Cerba on my way to the door. "Let's get some fresh air."

I believed she understood me when we both exited the lab.

Outside, my hair swayed wild with the cold wind. I tightened my jacket over my chest, watching Cerba running fiercely in the direction of the spooky forest, where some trees were devoid of foliage, if it wasn't for the crows perched on their branches.

She stopped a few meters away from me, her eyes stuck on the forest. Hugo came out of it a few seconds later. He was running toward the manor. By looking at him, you'd never have thought we were in the middle of winter. He wore only a gray shirt and shorts accompanying the landscape whose colors had lost their warmth, vivid and flamboyant touch, lowering the saturation to a grayish scenery. Hugo's ripped muscles were covered in sweat like he had trained underneath a burning sun for hours.

"Well, someone is in a mood," he exclaimed, stopping his run when he approached us.

"Well, somebody was a rude jerk to—"

"I was talking to Cerba," he cut off my grumbles and kneeled down in front of Cerba. She rushed to him, wagging her tail joyfully. He then lifted his eyes up to me. "But please, continue, *doudou.*"

"Never mind." I exhaled a sharp breath and examined the dry blood on Hugo's knuckles when he petted Cerba. He had bits of tree bark glued to his body with the sweat as if he had punched a tree Rocky style. "What's up with you, anyway?"

"Needed to chill. You know, channel my anger and all that shit." He shrugged.

"Why's that?"

"We all have our demons, right?" he answered with sincerity.

I nodded. *That we do.* He drew a flirty smile on his lips while annoying Cerba by teasing her to catch his fingers, which she was unsuccessful at doing.

"You know, you don't strike me as the kind of man who enjoys living in a reclusive manor," I hinted. "Why are you friends with Radcliff? You're nothing alike." Hugo was warm and friendly. He liked the spotlight and seemed like a passionate, careless man—the whole contrary of ruthless, calculated, mysterious Radcliff.

Hugo stood up, our stares connecting intensely. "I owe him my life. If it wasn't for him, I'd be dead."

"What?" I was dazed, my mouth hanging open.

He brushed it off. "It's a long story. The point is no one and nothing is black or white."

An awkward silence washed over us. In a couple of minutes, darker clouds had surrounded the sky, announcing an impending storm. I drew a misty, chilly breath before peering at Hugo, who was staring forcefully in the direction of the manor.

I reeled around to see what had captivated him and noticed a slight movement of the closed curtains on the balcony where Radcliff had stood on New Year's Eve. Was he observing us? At this thought, my heart galloped.

"You asked me once what kind of man Radcliff was?"

I held on to my breath, in a haze to know.

"I don't have an answer for you, but what I can tell you is that he saves lost souls," he stated.

Lost souls. That sentence resonated in my mind as I observed Hugo entering the gloomy manor. Cerba barked at me, giving me her puppy eyes, a huge branch carried in her mouth.

"Fine, let's play," I capitulated with a smile.

After all, this was why I was here. To play a game. The Devil's one.

Radcliff may or may not save souls, but I wondered about his. Could someone save his?

That would be a game I'm interested in winning.

Radcliff

I was peeking through the space between my curtains.

The wind was sweeping, whispering in the air that something bad was coming. The oak tree swayed, howling the sorrows it witnessed. My windows rattled forcefully, like a ghost wanting to escape the manor eagerly. Among all this pain stood a ray of light in the middle of the dark clouds spreading in the sky.

I look ridiculous. I stormed away, walking the hundred steps to my sinister office. My coat, like a cape, made the dust waltz in the air. Despite myself, I was cursed with curiosity. I came back to position, pushing the curtain slightly to peer one last time at her.

Her laugh was effortless and beautiful. Not that I could hear her, but the sound of it was impregnated inside my head. A ghost of a smile appeared momentarily on my face when I saw Lily hiding the stick inside her coat from Cerba. The poor dog was barking at her, jumping on her legs, full of excitement, hoping to catch it. She finally threw it away, Cerba sprinting like a fury after it.

I cleared my throat, realizing I was enjoying this scenery much more than I should. She was stealing my dog from me and not focusing on her job. If she thought I hadn't seen what she pulled off with Patrick earlier... My lips curled into a thin line at this thought, betraying my brain.

The sky opened up suddenly, unleashing a cascade of pouring rain on them. Anyone with some common sense would have taken shelter inside the manor.

Everyone but her.

She welcomed the rain on her skin, remaining stoic. She raked a hand through her sleek hair, shutting her eyes as if she were under a warm shower.

"What is she playing?" I rumbled.

The air outside was cold and numbing. Of course, Cerba joined her in her dementia. It was hard to tell who had enticed who. The both of them spun around, playing with the elements.

Lily danced like a flower goddess, a sorceress making my heart thunder. She moved her arms and delicate fingers with grace. Her hips rolled fiercely, matching her hair flying with passion. Wild and playful, she had no idea the effect she would have on any man. Lightning struck. Rain poured harder. My throat became tighter. My pupils grew darker. My throbbing erection transformed me into a madman.

There was something about her.

She had a spark of magic within her. The ability for her passion to burst into flames and to lighten the darkest of the skies.

The song of the exquisitely tormented weather matched her spirit and my heartbeats. I fisted my curtain with a strong grip, transported by each of her movements. Blood hissed to my head. I was on the verge of losing control when her eyes met mine from afar.

The sight of me made her stop—probably with disgust. Her pouty lips parted; the knot in my throat tightened. I must have looked like a beastly perv watching her.

But Lily waved in my direction with the brightest smile. A part of me doubted that this gesture was directed at me. But there was no one else around. My muscles contracted, and yet I still wasn't closing the damn curtain. Her smile faded slowly at the view of my frozen and impenetrable stare to her warmth.

I finally pulled away from the window and stopped this nonsense. I had to end this fantasy. I escaped my office, cracking my knuckles. I descended through the stairs, wishing to distract my mind at my library. Fighting my thoughts lately was one of the hardest things. Since her arrival, she had ingrained herself everywhere, disturbing my peace.

Speaking of her. Lily barged into my hallway like a kid who had been chased after, Cerba following right after her. Her laugh echoed throughout the whole manor. I gunned my eyes at my dog, who was smiling at me with her tongue hanging out. *Traitress.*

My eyes dipped down and lingered on the drops of water falling on my marble floor from her soaking wet coat. Her shoes, full of dirt, dispatched brown mud everywhere. And she couldn't care less.

Mrs. Walton would be delighted to know there was a child inside this house.

"Hi," Lily greeted. "I'm sorry for the mess. I can clean this up."

"I have people for that."

Shockingly, I liked things done in a certain way. I tolerated some deviations from the original plan, but Lily had the gift of turning everything upside down, of creating constant disorder. Surprisingly, I loathed it to the same degree it pleased me.

I strolled back in the direction of the library, hoping to find peace—if not, I would gaze at the transparency of her clothes underneath her coat.

"Wait. Where—What are you doing?" Her eyes went round, preventing me from advancing one more step. They flickered with interest, almost impossible to be detached to. "I just thought we could talk. Learn to get to know each other better, you know. After all, we're going to spend some time together."

I was near thunderstruck. First of all, because I had no desire to spend more time with her for both of our sakes. Second of all, because no one was foolish enough to wish to get to know me better. She was suicidal, and I was close to succumbing to my compulsions by mounting her like a caveman right here, right now.

"Radcliff hasn't told you yet?" Hugo appeared from the living room, intruding himself into the conversation.

I narrowed my eyes on him. *What the—*

Her lips pulled in an O shape. "Tell me what?"

"That he's inviting you to dinner tonight."

What the fucking hell? A vortex of anger swirled inside me. My knuckles cracked again. If anyone else disturbed or meddled with my privacy, they'd bitterly regret their choice, but Hugo couldn't be taught to have any decency in terms of manners. This time, he took it a step too far.

"Really?" Her eyes shone over me. *Wait.* Did she want this? Not that it mattered.

My mouth set in a hard line. "Eight p.m. Don't be late."

"I won't. Well, I better shower." She ran up the stairs, raindrops following her passage.

A muscle in my jaw twitched, my eyes ridden with anger. Each of my muscles tightened, so much so that I could feel my scar re-opening. I waited for her to leave before I whirled on Hugo.

"What the fuck do you think you're doing?" I shouted.

"I saw you spying on the cute witch earlier. She seemed lonely, and I thought—"

"And that's not your fucking place, Hugo."

He swallowed, avoiding my hellish stare by glancing at the ground.

"Try something like that one more time and you'll sorely regret it."

"I'm sorry, Radcliff, okay? I acted impulsively." A curse she seemed to put on everyone here. "I can tell her that—"

"No," I said coldly and probably too eagerly, feeling my rage dissipate.

Hugo let out a warm grin despite himself. It wasn't a date. It wouldn't be one.

"And get me in touch with Patrick Delange," I added.

I had something planned for him.

Chapter 12

Lily

Eight p.m. at the manor looked like the witching hour.

My heels echoed on the marble floor. My pastel blue skater skirt moved smoothly with the cold air of the hallway. The naked skin of my collarbone that wasn't hidden by my cotton pull shivered. The hair on my neck under my ponytail hissed.

Arriving at the dining area, I took in the big gothic chandeliers that hung over the long oval table serving different gastronomical dishes inside silver plates. It even had a chocolate fountain. A smile lit up my face. It was over-the-top, a buffet of luxury as if the host wanted to make sure his guest would remember this dinner.

Speaking of the host, I could only perceive Radcliff's shadow from where he stood at the other end of the table. A part of his body was illuminated by the cracking fire of the chimney, matching the atmosphere of the candles shining in the darkness. It was intimate.

If Radcliff wasn't who he was, it could even be perceived as a romantic date. A date with Dracula, when you end up being the meal.

He stepped forward to join me, coming out of the shadows so I could observe him more closely. He pulled out my chair in silence, his suit clinging tight to strong biceps. It would be a lie to say my heart wasn't thumping wildly in my chest. Radcliff always wore black, but tonight, he did it with a particular sophistication. His glossy raven hair was slicked back with hairspray. The refined cufflinks on his dress shirt glinted like small diamonds. His purple calla lily stare held the power to sweep the air from the room, forcing me to breathe his oxygen. Even the way he wore his scar that inked into his skin, like a thorny fortress closing in on a spell that had been made once upon a time, was magnetic.

"Did you do all of this?" My eyes lingered on everything but him, but my nostrils were drawn to him. His scent was a shelter to my soul, attracting every bone in me.

"Does it matter?" He sat in front of me in his king's chair. In one smooth movement of his hand, classical music started to play in the background.

"Of course it does." I sat at my place before unfolding my napkin and putting it over my legs. "This is nice. Almost like—" *You like me.* I bit the next words from my lips, feeling a flush creeping up my cheeks. "You're just hard to read," I added.

"So are you." Radcliff roamed my face, our eyes colliding with the same questioning.

"You know, I never had a one-on-one dinner with a man other than my uncle." I played with the silver cutlery, seeing my reflection in it. "It's a bit impressive." Especially since my first was with the scariest of all.

"Then, I suppose, I won't need to worry about a boyfriend of yours."

My heart leaped violently in my throat when a sardonic

knife-sharp grin appeared on Radcliff's lips—half-terrifying, half-threatening.

"No. I —" I abruptly laid the fork back on the table, sucking in all the air. "I don't have a boyfriend. Why would you need to worry, anyway?"

"I want you dedicated to your task." He paused, holding his glass between his fingers. He moved the red garnet wine slightly like a bloody sea. "Plus, the sooner you're done, the sooner we can both get back to our lives." *Right.* "How did the meeting go with Patrick today?"

"Fine," I lied, intertwining my fingers together under the table to hide my nervousness.

"I saw you. I know what happened."

He sipped his glass calmly, in contradiction to his glacial tone that froze my insides. I wanted to defend myself. To reply that I'd get the job done despite our disagreement. I needed the Devil's Corpse to make my perfume more than anything in the world, and something in my gut screamed that Radcliff wouldn't be as lenient with me if I started posing problems with his staff. But I couldn't speak. Maybe the sisters were right. I was vain and too proud.

His mouth set in a grim line. "Do you know what I said to Patrick?"

"It won't happen again," I excused myself.

"I told him…" He stopped, and my heartbeat echoed in my chest loudly. "I told him he'd do as you please. That you're the one deciding." Radcliff kept his stare on me, probably aware of the way my eyes had widened. "So you can expect your oils to be delivered this week and whatever else you need. I believe you had a list?"

"What? You defended me?" I was breathless. Patrick was a respected man with more experience than I—how could he have chosen me instead?

"I can be very convincing when I want something, little witch.

As much as I can be very cruel when I don't obtain it." A ghost of a smile spread over his face. The kind of smile where you don't want to be the victim of Radcliff's wrath.

"I don't understand... I mean, why—"

"From now on, I want you to believe in yourself. Don't disappoint me."

"You truly believe in me?" A warm feeling filled my belly. It was butterflies. I was touched by his words despite the spite in them. Perhaps because apart from my mother, no one ever truly did. Perhaps because Radcliff's approval was so hard to gain that it meant more.

"That doesn't matter either. You'll never achieve anything if you let anyone dictate what you can or cannot do."

"I don't," I tried to convince myself. "People and their words don't get to me."

"I don't like liars," he countered. "You use your pride to pretend to be untouchable, but you'll just end up mediocre doing so. Don't deny what's inside of you. Use it. Use everything. The good and the bad. If you want to create something exceptional, you can't lie with your feelings."

"Says the man known to not have an ounce of humanity," I shot back, knowing he was right. Lying wasn't just about words. It was about denial. Denying your emotions, being a coward to them. But letting the truth out was far more dangerous and painful sometimes.

"Which says a lot about me," he mocked.

A bad feeling crept down my spine as long as a strange fascination. Radcliff had used his feelings to create his empire, until none remained inside of him. Until he had reached the status of excellence. He belonged to the category I coveted.

"So, you were human, once upon a time." Our eyes connected, and I took the first bite of the white truffle among the red meat and pretentious vegetables—the gourmet kind, served with colors and savors. "What happened?"

"Maybe I'm just born this way."

I smiled. "Evil isn't born. It's made. Just like inhumanity. It's all about choices." Usually, the greatest of the villains had to sacrifice the person they loved the most to gain their ultimate power. They sacrificed their biggest strength—their heart.

"To choices." He raised his glass to make a toast.

I did the same, entrapped by the depths in his eyes. I tasted the alcohol I swore to never drink. The liquid corrupted my lips. The red cherry and leather notes infused my nostrils. He took another first from me.

The rest of the dinner was filled with a blossoming silence. Not the heavy silence you want to escape from, but the strangely appeasing one that intensifies the present moment. The one which leaves the floor to our souls, letting them share much more privacy than just words.

Sometimes, we would swivel our eyes toward each other. In the midst of this otherworldly atmosphere, nervousness surged in my veins. I bet he felt it too, that invisible pull that pushed us further toward the other. The way his eyes dipped down and lingered on my lips could have fooled me for attraction—if he wasn't him. But he couldn't possibly want me.

By the end of dinner, Radcliff rose up without a word and ambled toward me. I got up from my seat, our bodies almost colliding, with only a few inches separating us. That proximity was enough for a bolt of electricity to travel between us. *Vanilla*. I turned my gaze away under the smell of the new scent I'd picked up. Radcliff's odor was attractive to me. Too attractive, that each note lured me into his darkness.

"Why are you afraid of the dark?" he asked genuinely with the rasp of his voice.

What happened with the sisters and my wicked childhood was my secret. And if anyone could understand the burden of burying secrets in the most secluded part of our mind, it would probably be Radcliff.

"For the same reason you fear light," I mused. "The unknown."

"You're mistaking me for one of your mythical creatures."

"I fear monsters in the dark. But you, you fear to be under the spotlight. To be discovered for who you truly are. To be seen. Unraveled." I was convinced he was playing a twisted game for an outcome no one had known. "No one throws exuberant parties and is not a part of it."

I jutted my chin up and let him observe me. The way he clenched his jaw, his stare firmly set on me, betrayed that I was in the right.

"You don't know anything about me, nor my fears," he replied, his voice laced with bitterness.

"So what do you fear, then?"

Radcliff would have left if my fingertips hadn't grazed his hand gripping the chair by mistake. If that innocent touch hadn't created a thundering sensation inside my core, I'd have taken a step back. But I didn't. It enticed him to look back to me, and me to hold my hand behind my back. Tingling dissipated from my fingers to my palm.

"Water." He ascended into a murderous rasp. "The water of that cliff is cursed. And if you continue to ask so many questions, you will be too."

In a flash, he left through the dim edges, leaving only the memory of his magnetic, manly scent.

Radcliff was wrong.

He was cursed.

Chapter 13

LILY

"What are you doing?" Radcliff's hostile stare encountered mine through his book.

Even his antipathetic tone couldn't erase the huge beam on my face. I had no doubts I was disturbing whatever free time he had and wanted to spend it in peace. Radcliff was sitting crossed-legged on his black leather sofa, Cerba sleeping at his feet. Dressed in another of his black suits, he analyzed my outfit doubtfully.

"It's my tulip dress," I replied to his stare, brushing my fingers over the dress, playing with it.

He closed his book, his thumb rubbing over his lips as if he was trying to know what the heavens I meant by that. His gaze lingered on my bustier under my vest coat, then on the tutu shape of my puffy knee-length dress.

"You know, because it looks like a tulip. A reverse one if you look upside down," I explained, bowing my head to the side to actually look at it from an upside-down angle.

Clearly, we didn't have the same symbolism in tulips. For me, it was a joyful hint to the color of love in pink shades. For him, it was an incredulous haze of gray, even though a slight snarl drew on his lips. I couldn't tell if he found me amusing or, on the contrary, he liked it in his own way.

He opened his book again, wearing his impassive mask like a crown once more. "And why are you wearing that dress?"

"Because we are going for a walk."

He didn't share my elation.

The point was, after the crisp, stormy days, the sunlight had appeared. I had decided it was the perfect time for a walk while waiting for the delivery of the oils. Plus, I couldn't stay alone in this gloomy manor. Truth was, I wasn't that alone. I had a friend. A flower. But I was determined to pretend that my host actually wanted me here and to force him into sharing a normal afternoon with me—even if neither of us were normal individuals.

"You can do as you please. You aren't a prisoner, and you don't need my approbation." His attention focused back on his book, deliberately ignoring my enthusiasm.

"I said 'we.'" I always thought that my dream was the only area for my stubbornness to act upon. Apparently, piercing Radcliff's persona was one of them too. "I want to walk with you." My voice quivered when I pronounced *you*.

Radcliff's stare went back on me, his eyebrows furrowed as if he was facing a dilemma.

I was eager to add, "You know, I don't know the area that well. I wouldn't want to lose myself." Which was partly true—the phone GPS was a nightmare around here.

"You can take Cerba."

For some unknown reason, I cared. I cared that he refused me. I jutted my chin up. "Fine."

I left the living room, fuming. Cerba followed right after me, running wildly through the windswept manor. A burning fire was growing inside of me. Irritation skittered across my nerves. Passing through the hallway, I forced a smile at Mr. and Mrs. Walton, who were standing like statues near the stairs. Their constant silence created only bitterness. At first, I thought they were haunted ghosts. Now, I wondered if I wasn't the problem.

I stepped away, creaking open the imposing gate before I crept through the misty forest. It was foolish of me to think I would solve my isolation through the company of nature, even if it did work before. I inhaled the magical smell of pine, golden amber, and balsam fir, carrying me into a wonderland where I was free of mind.

Sinking deeper into the woods, I found a world that has been forgotten by humankind, pure and untouched. Birdsong came in bursts like a lullaby, and Cerba chased after a few rabbits. I was lost in time. The sun had bloomed in the sky, peeking through the tree branches. Light and shadow danced across my face.

The expanse of trees ahead of us was never-ending. I was surrounded in the belly of the woods, and looking back, there were many ways back.

I was lost.

"Don't go too far, Cerba." I pulled out my phone to check where I was while continuing to advance. A pointless act since the connection was nonexistent.

A cracking noise breached the peaceful forest.

I'd have stumbled if it wasn't for someone who had grabbed my arm fiercely, making me turn around. My eyes fluttered shut, and I crashed brutally against a strong torso. My heart thumped harder when I smelled a woody scent, intoxicating my nostrils and filling my lungs.

The songs of the forest stopped as if it had become lifeless by the sole presence of him. It became a cold realm, welcoming a merciless king. My fingers instinctively grazed his strong biceps, and I braved to swivel my eyes to him. Captured in the moment, our stares and souls joined. I swore by losing myself in Radcliff's firestorm eyes, they told a somber story.

I could see beyond the scars he wore.

I wasn't horrified. He wasn't god-awful. For a moment, I found Radcliff's beauty rare in a sinister way, and a new form of desire blossomed in my belly. The Devil was playing a trick on me.

"What are you doing?" I blurted, pulling away from him, confusion clouding my head.

"You were about to step into an animal trap."

Radcliff threw a piece of wood inside the trap. I flinched when it closed brutally, breaking the baton. I imagined what would have happened to me if I'd taken one more step.

"Thank you," I huffed.

"Don't thank me—just be more careful. You can't trust everything." His voice was threatening yet somehow worried.

I nodded. Radcliff passed in front of me, and I hurried to join him as the forest engulfed him into its blackness. From time to time, we'd peer secretly over at each other. I felt like a shy teenager, my body reacting in a way I never thought it would.

I suddenly paid attention to my posture, trying to look attractive for him. My fingers brushed the plants elegantly. Each of my steps and gestures seemed to be enchanted by fairy dust. Using the branches of the trees, I hid my gaze from him. I peered over him like he was my secret, observing him closely.

When his eyes met mine, I smiled and turned away, hoping he wouldn't perceive my thoughts. My heart pounded, a wave of heat warming me through the cold. Even the scent I was smelling was different. My wonderland became a bright and floral fairy tale.

It created the illusion of the sweet scent of spring gardens, ylang-ylang, and enchanted roses.

Radcliff was imposing, a constant frown on his face accompanying a squared jaw, a Grecian nose, and broad shoulders. So tenebrous that even his tall shadow on the grass was somehow scary. Nothing about him belonged here. And yet, seeing him in my universe for the first time enlivened my soul. I wondered if in another life we'd met.

Beyond the immensity of the trees stood a gigantesque valley. It felt like we went through a secret passage between two universes. A smile painted my face at the dappled light matching the meek blue sky.

From afar, we could see an abandoned church or an old chapel, judging by the cross on top of it. It was in dreadful shape, the walls of stones broken up. Growing trees and ivy were swallowing the roof.

I was intrigued. "What is it?"

"Something that belongs to the past." Radcliff's jaw tightened at the sight of it.

I took an impulsive step toward it, like I was magnetically attracted. I looked back to see that Radcliff wasn't following me. "You aren't coming?"

Silence flew over us before he resigned himself to walk behind me.

From the outside, the church was meaningless. Ruined. Ugly. But when I wrenched open the old door, it wasn't what I expected.

It was beautiful.

Some empty spaces where windows would have stood before were now sharp, with shattered pieces of glass lying on the floor. The candles for people to make a prayer on were covered in dust. What struck me the most was the remaining stained-glass window of a biblical scene. It portrayed forgiveness. The colors reflected on the floor, painting the inside of the church with prime colors shining through the crystal like a rainbow.

I whirled around through the beam of colors, the spots dancing on my face. "Isn't it beautiful?"

Feeling dizzy, I stopped, facing Radcliff. He was glaring at the whole place, crossing his arms on his chest. I didn't think he even heard me. His lips twitched downward, his stare fixed on a pew where once upon a time people would have made prayers. The flames of hell flashed in his eyes as if he was transported to a memory haunting him.

I stepped alongside him and stroked his fingers with mine in a ghost of a touch. "Do you know this place?"

"I did," he answered solemnly, forcing a Machiavellian smirk on his face. "My father would drag me here on Sundays."

I observed more closely the place, trying to enter Radcliff's head. My gaze stuck on the stained glass. I had seen it before inside Radcliff's club. It was the same scenery but a different type of worship. Club 7 depicted the sins and everything unholy, and it took inspiration from... this place.

"Was he a good man?" I asked.

"To God's blind eyes, yes." *But not for you.*

It was all an illusion.

Everything about Radcliff was.

We were all blind in front of him. We spoke tales, yet no one knew who he truly was.

"Is that why you have that card? The Devil?" The pieces of the puzzle of Radcliff were starting to come together in my mind. "Is it for revenge?"

He parted from me, looming closer to the stained glass. "Not quite. You can't take revenge on who you are. Your identity." He chuckled with a sinister laugh. "Perhaps we're suffering the same torment, Lily."

I gulped, and he continued his walk across the church. Radcliff, too, wanted to be greater than life. Instead of becoming light, he became death and shadows. Instead of leaving an imprint on Earth, he left one in hell.

"Obsession," I spoke in a suffocated whisper.

That's how our universes collided together. His demonic one in quest of an aphrodisiac and mine for a heavenly fragrance. My hope and his inhumanity in an eternal battle.

"You know, I grew up with the sisters of the charity. But I never found my place there."

Radcliff's attention was suddenly on me. I clamped my fingers into my flesh. All these years, I'd never confessed. And today, I would. To the Devil and his church of the night.

"I was taught I was never alone, but I always felt lonely. Abandoned somehow." My voice was creaking and tight. My throat closed as if I was forbidden to speak those words. "I wanted to believe, but all I felt was pain like I'd never matter to anyone. It was a nightmare. I never had something that was only mine, you know? Except for my dream."

I didn't know why I was confiding in him something I never dared to bring up to anyone. Probably because he could understand me. I took my pain, my sorrows, my fears, and from there I became water, fighting the deadly fire that was tormenting me.

"I thought I'd resent this kind of place, but I don't. Like I said—"

"There is beauty in the ugly," he finished.

And just like that, our ugliness met, forming a strong bond.

And most importantly, I found Radcliff's light.

A heart that could someday beat again.

Chapter 14

Lily

I was too hot.

The humidity amplified the feeling of the sweat running down my skin. I was trying to catch my breath, which was echoing through the amber room. The crackle of the burning candles, like a hellfire, flared wildly in a sunset landscape.

I'm burning.

My senses on hyperalert, I touched my forehead, wondering if I wasn't inside a sauna. I closed my eyes, smelling saffron and sandalwood. I was spinning like I had a heavy sunburn. Losing my equilibrium, I pulled open my eyelids.

Desire grew in my belly. The shadow of a man ambled in my direction. Each of his steps made the earth shake, the room narrowing under his presence. My sight was blurry—I had to squint to see him closer.

His body was tinted in a fire color. It displayed well-defined abs with drops of sweat sliding through them to his black trousers. My throat became dry as I admired the epitome of power and strength. I was in turmoil, my gaze stuck on his hunky biceps.

But, in a flash, he vanished into thin air. Or so I thought until I felt a scorching breeze behind me, an invisible presence making each of my cells rattle.

"You're mine, little witch," the Devil whispered behind my ear.

Radcliff.

His calloused hand untied the knot of my dress, which fell to the ground and turned to ashes. I was naked when he seized my waist possessively, his lips enchanting my neck. Being unraveled and offered to him, I left my inhibitions behind, and my primal instinct shone. I was falling deeper inside a tornado of lust.

The heat inflamed me. His fingers brushed to my center, my hips moving to his control. My neck craned when his other hand pulled my hair backward for his lips to possess me. He sealed his darkness on me, waving his tongue across mine. He touched me like no one else had before, stroking his fingers on my sex. New cravings blossomed in me. I was wet under the torrid heat, entering into a vortex of sins.

"Let me possess you the way you want me to," Radcliff enticed to my ear.

I took that as an order, my body enslaved by him. The way he rubbed his fingers on me created an explosion of glowing fireworks inside me. I wanted to scream, bolts of pleasure coursing the length of my core. Orgasm, bliss, and lust—I was addicted.

He whirled me around, carrying me effortlessly to a velvet bed. He towered over top of me while I unfastened his fly, liberating his hardness. I surrendered to his powerful aura, and he parted my legs, seizing my thighs to pull me closer to him.

"I want you," I moaned, struggling to breathe.

He devoured my body with his hands and sucked on my nipples. Playing me like a symphony, his tongue was a work of art, making my back arch under each of his flicks. He delivered the final music note by rolling my nipples between his forefingers. Goose bumps spread on my skin despite the heat. He stuck me between heaven and hell.

I was entrapped by the purple of his gaze. It formed a bouquet of black calla lilies for me, and diving deeper into it, I felt like our souls had merged, as if we could read each other's secrets.

His stare worshipped me, granting me the status of goddess, but his dominating touch showed he'd never let me back to the gods' world. I belonged with him.

He cuffed my wrists with a strong grip, his searing stare erasing all traces of purple to darken even more. I bit my lower lip, loving being at his mercy. My legs beseeched him, opening slowly.

"Let out your darkness, Lily. Show who you truly are," he said, hot and threatening.

I'm burning. His hard sex entered me without warning, my whole core responding to him with twice the intensity he gave me. As he thrust harder and deeper, the strength of his desire for me was inhuman. It was beyond everything. Chaos engendering earth. The flames of the room enveloped us, as if we were in the middle of a fire.

I saw red. I dug my nails down his hand, and in response, he caged me deeper against him with a kiss. Our lips collided, exchanging our missing breath. The softness of his lips was a lie compared to the harshness of his thrusts.

I sucked on them like an addict, savoring the taste of pomegranates on his lips. I craved more, like a mythical creature craving blood. My carnal desire had transformed me into someone else. Radcliff tried to pull away, but my mouth invaded his.

I bit him.

Blood dissipated from his lips like pomegranate juice.

I drank it, mad for the taste, sucking on it as much as I could.

Then the blood stopped, and Radcliff inched backward from me. His lips curled into a satisfying snarl, cruel and wicked, when he drilled his infernal eyes into me. His scar reflected his blackness, spreading over his face like ink-venom. His features darkened, and the light in the room dimmed. A shiver traveled the length of my spine.

"You can't escape me, Lily."

Lily…

Lily…

The rasp of his voice prickled at my senses, resonating in my mind like the shadows calling me.

My eyes fluttered open. My thumping heart slowed down. The heat was gone, the sheets of my bed soaked. The rising sun poured through the tree branches, casting a rosy hue across the sky.

It was all a dream.

Or a nightmare.

I took a walk across the garden to overshadow my thoughts and find peace. Around me, everything was quiet. Even the ravens and the foliage went silent in an inner meditation. I was surprised to not witness Mr. and Mrs. Walton's ghostly presence, nor Radcliff's chilling aura. *Radcliff.* My pulse throated in my neck, my cheeks reddening at the remembrance of the salacious dream I had last night.

Damn you, Lily.

Luckily for me, Radcliff wasn't the type to hang by the

greenhouse during the day. I was in a safe territory to let my dream vanish from my memory.

The calm was interrupted by Cerba's barking leaping above the sound of water, probably coming from a hose.

I ambled in her direction to see what the fuss was about. Positioning myself behind the cypress hedge, I glanced at Cerba covered in dirt, moving her tail with joyful interest. She looked like she had rolled herself in a muddy hole. I pushed the branches slightly to give me a better view while remaining hidden. Someone was seated behind her.

Wait—Radcliff?

"I can't believe you're enjoying this," Radcliff grunted to Cerba while cleaning her up with the hose and soap.

Soulless, terrifying, insensitive Radcliff—or so he pretended to be—was taking care of little and adorable Cerba. My heart thundered. Never in my wildest thoughts would I have imagined that. I witnessed him roaming his masculine hands over Cerba's hair, taking care of her like a precious child.

"I didn't teach you to behave like that." Obviously, he still had a way with words. "You better stop smiling. It won't happen twice."

I inched silently to the right with the desire to have a better view without either of them noticing me. I couldn't help the huge beaming smile on my face, knowing this was a moment he'd want to keep secret. With Radcliff's profile finally visible, I had found the perfect angle until silly me had to step on a branch, attracting their attention.

I felt like the earth had crumbled at my feet when Radcliff turned around for our stare to join. My heartbeat stopped. Time slowed. Danger flickered in each part of him. His eyes, marbled with chaos, transported me into his dark realm. His thick eyebrows dipped dangerously. A strand of his wet raven hair dropped bad-boyishly on his forehead.

I drilled my gaze to his wet, half-opened pitch-black dress shirt. The fabric clung tight to his well-defined muscles. The drops of water flowed down his strong chest. He had the body of an Olympic god, proudly wearing the scars of his past.

I was attracted to Radcliff in a messy, incomprehensible kind of way.

Behind the ugly and cold mask he wore, I discovered his rare beauty. It wasn't in a conventional way. No. It was the powerful charisma that inhabited him.

The way my soul unquestionably craved his scent, an aroma of sandalwood and vanilla—my fear for him felt like a dangerous aphrodisiac. A growing fascination inhabited me. An admiration even. The feeling that I could be more than sweet Lily.

It was chemical.

"Lily."

At the sound of his voice, I remembered the way his fingertips caressed my skin. The way he possessed my soul and body in my dreams. I swallowed my thoughts, the burning heat inflaming me once more.

"You look flushed," he added, a sly grin hinting he could read my thoughts.

But that was impossible—or maybe not. After all, he was Radcliff: the word "impossible" didn't seem to exist for him.

Just when I wondered if we had shared the same dream, his eyes scooped down my body and lingered, making me feel like an open book to him. More than reading through me, he had the power to write the following pages.

"No, I… Um…" *Way to go, Lily.*

My skin flushed with embarrassment. Luckily, Cerba came to my distress, shaking the water off her and splashing Radcliff with drops. I scooped down to pet her, taking this opportunity to change the subject. "What did you do, cutie, huh?"

"She thought she could befriend a rabbit. Moral of the story, she scared him to death, dirtying herself," Radcliff stated coldly.

"She's lonely. She just wanted to play," I defended her, her puppy eyes piercing my soul. My heart melted for the rabbit; he didn't deserve to have his life taken away, but I understood Cerba. Loneliness can be tough.

"And she did, at the price of the rabbit's life. There's always a price to pay. That's why some beings are better off alone."

Now I was convinced we weren't talking about Cerba anymore.

"I disagree. No one should be alone."

His eyes sliced straight to mine.

"I mean, I've always been apart. Solitary. I haven't experienced many things. My life has been pretty boring and plain, just like me." I overshared with Radcliff, who had a perplexed expression on his face.

"You're far from it," he deadpanned.

My heart skipped a beat, locking my eyes with his. "What do you know?"

A growing silence settled between us. A pulsation in me was yearning to be held by Radcliff, but I refrained. The wind suddenly rose, coming out of its silence. A breeze pulled me toward him, and almost instinctively, we inched forward. The dead leaves circled us, swirling around in a tango.

Nature had awoken for me what I tried to bury underneath myself.

Our breaths connected in symbiosis. The few inches separating us were fatal. I bit my lower lip in apprehension of the kiss to come. I saw in his eyes the craving he had, his dilated pupils prompting me to surrender to chaos. Radcliff was a silent volcano at the verge of explosion, and when it did, it'd be destructive.

He then pulled away, stood up, and clenched his hand. Radcliff regained his icy expression, shooting me a last glance. "You'll see tonight. Be ready at eight. We're going to the opera."

That was a date.

It was incontestably a beautiful day.

I even thought Mrs. Walton had given me a smile earlier when I ran across the stairs. I roamed my room with excitement, my toes making the flooring creak. I whirled around, drunk with the idea of a night out. I imagined the splendor of the opera in each of my steps. Gaining momentum with my spins, I fell over my bed, feeling dizzy.

I distinguished a small packet next to me and drew a smile. Posed delicately on the bed, it was wrapped in a ballet-slipper-pink gift wrap. I got up on my knees and hastened to read the majestic card on top of it. It reverberated in the light, the shiny black background covered with real gold forming a flower pattern. The writing was regal and elegant, like a royal invitation.

Because a flower goddess deserves her own crown.

Butterflies blossomed in my belly as I repeated my new nickname in a whisper. *Flower goddess*. That name felt like a spring breeze sweeping me across the most enchanting places in the universe, perching in the highest of clouds.

That packet could only come from one man. The one who spoke little but captured my soul between his words. The one who was infamous but capable of beauty. The one who despised mortals just called me goddess.

Radcliff.

Unpacking the gift, I laid eyes upon the most beautiful and luxurious thing I'd ever seen in my entire life.

A precious jewel.

A hair brooch fit for a queen.

The most dazzling lily.

I took the hair jewel between my palms. Sparkling diamonds were spread like a sumptuous liana that would clip like a bridal hairpin. I grazed the white-gold lilies added to this elegant design, along with small pearls forming little flowers at the end.

It was the first thing I owned that was entirely mine. It was certainly expensive but, most incredibly, custom-made especially for me. Radcliff had translated my soul with disturbing ease. It was more than a simple gift; it was a message illustrating the power of the interest he conveyed to me.

I hurried to the mirror and fixed the brooch in my hair. A flush crept on my face as I watched my reflection. I combed my hair, running my fingers through it, feeling like a recently hatched butterfly. Wearing something from Radcliff triggered a strange sensation in me.

I felt special.

I should forbid an attraction with him. It was the most uncanny of scenarios. We were two opposites whose dreams intertwined together for a messy outcome. But as I spent time with him, I was convinced I could reach out to his humanity and make him change his mind about the aphrodisiac and the dark schemes he had in mind for it.

My phone rang, and I blanched. I was no longer looking at my reflection but at the name of the caller. My uncle. I hastened to pick up.

"My Lily, I'm so sorry it took me so long to reply. Please, forgive me. How are you?" he asked. "Radcliff isn't too monstrous with you?"

I simpered in my bed, a coy smile on my face, still on my cloud. "He isn't like I was expecting, Uncle. He's actually..." *Charming.* "Not that bad. And that flower, Uncle? It's amazing! Well, obviously, I don't approve of what he wants." *A weapon of extreme desire for personal gains.* "But when you get to know Radcliff, he's—"

"Wait, what?" Uncle Eugene howled. "You don't get to know a man like him. He doesn't care about you, Lily, nor anyone."

"That's not true. He invited me tonight to an opera and got me this incredible—"

"Lily," he huffed. "He's manipulating you and probably wants only one thing from you."

"No." A cold shiver traveled through my spine. Radcliff could have touched me without my consent or hurt me, and he hadn't. "You have to believe me, Uncle. I know there is good in him."

"Have you seen his face, Lily? He's hideous." He snorted. "A beautiful girl like you should pay attention to a guy like Adonis, not that creature."

"He's not hideous," I bit out. "If he's as bad as you tell me, why did you leave me with him? You didn't even call me back!"

My heart was pounding. My uncle remained silent, facing the venom of my words. Seconds became a loud minute, and a knot appeared in my throat. I swallowed it away, regretting having yelled at him.

"I'm sorry, Uncle. I gotta go. Please, let me know—"

"I didn't mean to leave you with him, I had no choice. I couldn't face you and tell you that... I've failed you. That man has no soul. I never wanted that for you," he pleaded with growing desperation. "Be careful with the influence he's having on you. You don't sound like my sweet Lily, the one that I know and raised."

You didn't raise me. The sisters did while I waited for you to pick me up for the holidays.

"I hope you'll find yourself back. Talk soon."

He hung up.

I was finding myself again.

Perhaps, I could be more than floral, sweet, and plain Lily. Spring fragrances had shaped who I was, but that wasn't all.

Perhaps, I could be a seductive aroma of a midnight dream, mystical and voluptuous. An oriental scent of patchouli, precious woods, and cinnamon from the Middle East. The mysterious lands of jasmine and vanilla. The animalistic and captivating tones, accompanied by the scents of myrrh and plum.

Perhaps, I'd been wearing the wrong fragrance on my soul all along.

Chapter 15

Radcliff

We're going to the opera.

A knife under my throat would have been nothing under the torture I was exposing myself to voluntarily. And now, here I was, the sound of my steps resonating through the long hallway and my words stuck on my jaw, sneering at my lack of judgment.

I tucked my tarot set inside my vest pocket, in case business needed to be done, and adjusted my midnight-black jacket. If it wasn't for the full moon shimmering through the imposing windows, no light would spark inside the dim corridor. Walking faster at the view of the vestibule, I cleared my throat.

I was used to wearing an expensive five-piece suit and Italian loafers, but I'd never come to such events with a date. In fact, most of the time I sent Hugo to represent me. I was the Unseen one, after all. An unyielding ghost, unmoved by people's feelings. Coldhearted, they said.

The point of the story was, I had no clue why I'd invited her. She weakened me, fucking up my head with unwanted questions. I had to make a decision. The scenario where I'd steal her from her world was growing deeper in me. I yearned for sweet Lily to shine by my side, to curse them with her beauty just like she had cursed me.

Everyone I had business with would be there. I cracked my knuckles, imagining their delighted faces at the sight of me, and the headlines: "The monstrous Devil of Ravencliff, ladies and gentlemen, leaving the underworld."

Each of them, irrelevant as they were, would be thinking tonight that their exclusive invitation would guarantee them *The World*. It wasn't the truth. I'd seen in the cards the night would rule under *The Moon*.

Danger. Hidden enemies. Disgrace. *I can't wait for it.*

I checked my watch as I arrived at my front door. She was late. I stopped, crossed my arms, and tapped my foot impatiently. She was making me wait in my hallway like some teenager picking up his date for prom. I didn't like this. What the hell was happening to me?

Mrs. Walton passed in front of me with a warm smile on her face. I slightly quirked my eyebrows together, observing her engulfing herself in the darkness. She never smiled in my presence. The last time it happened, I was a weak boy. My heartbeat increased into a pounding of anger. Lily was changing too many things around here. They needed a reminder I was still the same monster.

The staircase squeaked, and my body froze into place like it had received an electric shock. My gaze sliced straight to Lily's hand, delicately posed on the rail, before roaming to her long legs as she started her descent. She was wearing high heels, and most unexpectedly, she was dressed in all black for the first time. Her silk dress curved to her form with elegance and charm. I adjusted my tie at the sight of her—she knew how to make an entrance.

Fuck me. Blood hissed into my pants, and I hid my throbbing erection by crossing my hands in front of my trousers. My body was rebelling against me. That damn witch. She was a sorceress, more beautiful than Aphrodite, more charismatic than Cleopatra. She wore an invisible crown, her eyes screaming of fire and power. Lily wasn't solely an angel. She became something darker and somehow magnified.

Sweet Lily took from Eve, but tonight she became Lilith.

"You're staring," she mused, finishing her descent to meet me. "Thank you for the jewel. It's beautiful. I'll always cherish it. You must have had a hard time finding something this perfect?"

I swore her lashes fluttered. She skimmed her fingers across the brooch tangled in her hair that she wore like a goddess. The illusion that she was mine built up, and the impulse to fist her hair and draw her into a kiss tore me apart.

"It's nothing."

I just scared the hell off some of the most well-known Parisian jewelers to have it made by tonight. Roared after them when those incompetents placed roses instead of lilies on the brooch. Then, I fired them. The perks of owning not only diamond companies but also being one of the top jewel companies, some people might think.

"Well, thank you again." She nibbled on her bottom lip.

For fuck's sake. A thirsty demon in my chest was increasing like a bad tumor with the need of possession. My dick kept on pulsing behind my zipper, an intense craving wanting me to brand her lips with mine, to fuck her senseless and take everything from her. Her heart. Her soul. Her essence. I wanted her to poison me, to spellbind me while I devoured every piece of her. My devastating compulsions yearned to be freed.

I wanted ownership.

To snatch her to heaven for us to plummet to hell.

She'd be the most exquisite form of self-destruction I could inflict on myself.

What the hell—I'd gone mad for that woman. I shouldn't fall for it.

"Black isn't your color." It was mine.

Her wearing it was a lie. It wasn't her. She didn't belong with me.

"Why?" She raised an eyebrow, parting her sultry, blood-red lips.

"You don't have the darkness for it. It doesn't fit you." *You're torturing me.*

"What do you know? Maybe I do."

She held my stare fiercely.

I smiled devilishly.

Tonight, I'd have a flower goddess and a wicked witch by my side.

L'Opéra Garnier was full of ghosts and tragic incidents.

From secret passages to the lake under the fifth basement, its somber history had created an excessive fascination. It wasn't the only haunted place, but luxury has its perks. Those being columns and grand staircases in the image of the Roman palaces, Neobaroque architecture filled with ornamentation and sculptures, flaming red curtains and lavish embellishment.

The crowd focused on taking selfies, putting on display the little wealth they had, and engaging in fake interest in conversations—the whole package with all kinds of smiles. Obviously, most of them stopped their socializing at our arrival.

The room filled with a loud silence, leaving the floor to the ghosts. I peered over Lily, whose hand tightened on my biceps, her nails digging through the fabric of my suit. Her dilated pupils couldn't hide the mask of panic on her face. You'd think she didn't like the spotlight, to shine under the gaze of the envious. But the way her chest rose and her skin bristled on her collarbone showed her excitement. Fearless and shy, she was a delicious combo.

The crowd stared. Gasped. Gossiped. Most of them had never dared to look me directly in the eyes, whether it was out of fear or disgust. After all, humans' eyes expel the ugly from their sight. Curiosity, on the contrary, was a sin they gladly gave in to.

And tonight, the most courageous ones tried—after all, it was a once-in-a-lifetime opportunity. But they soon drifted their gazes away, meeting the strength of my own. They twitched their lips into scared smiles, swallowing their cowardly thoughts.

But this time, it was different. I inspired not only awe and terror but envy. Not for my wealth. Not for my power. But because of Lily.

"Everyone is looking at us," Lily muttered.

"No. Everyone is looking at you." My eyes leered upon her, the words escaping my lips. "You look beautiful."

I quickly dropped my gaze, ignoring her gleaming eyes. We passed toward the crowd—needless to say, I was feeding her to the sharks. A few of my business partners nodded their heads at me, none of them stepping close to Lily. I read the discontentment of my presence through their politeness.

All the men ogled over her, craving what was mine without having any chance to defy me. Their impulses were nothing compared to my destructive one.

Women glared with jealousy at Lily, not having an ounce of her beauty and her passion.

The person by my side would be the most guarded of all tonight.

You don't steal what belongs to the Devil, or you'll have to face his punishment.

In the midst of all this tension, a voice I recognized resonated across the crowd. "Lily!"

The Carmin son had pulled Lily by her arm to make her face him. I held her back, keeping her by my side with a firm grip. He stumbled backward, letting go of Lily when his gaze snapped to mine, stunned.

Only then did Junior realize who she came with tonight. The pulse of his heart thudded in his throat before he reflexively looked at the floor. I held his daddy's stare from afar. Melissa was hanging on his arm in an outfit that revealed way too much for this kind of event. Her eyes narrowed, lingering on Lily.

"Adonis. Come back here," Christian ground out, clenching his teeth. The vein on his forehead swelled. *It looks like Junior is in trouble.*

But Carmin Jr. rebelled, not moving. I guess his attachment to Lily was stronger than I thought. Like he could be enough for her. He wasn't even a man.

"Adonis. It's great to see you here." Lily smiled genuinely, ignoring the sinful desire this prick had for her. "You know Radcliff?"

Like we needed an introduction. The absurdity of this scenario irritated me. Adonis held out his hand hesitantly. I darted my eyes to his gesture. It was only a matter of seconds before he pulled his hand back where it came from.

"Can I talk to you in private?" he whispered to Lily.

Lily turned to me with the purest smile. Her scent intoxicated my senses, and I already cursed the sentence that was coming.

"I'll be back," she assured me.

I watched her sweep away from me, loathing the idea of it. I acted on my impulse and held her wrist instinctively. I contained myself to not hurt her, keeping the need to knock down Junior in check.

"Two minutes," I said, my voice deadly.

I released her. I had no desire to leave Lily alone with Carmin Jr. People were watching, and I was on the verge of unleashing my wrath on anyone. She transformed me into a possessive, primal monster.

I ignored the spike of jealousy suffusing my veins for my own well-being. I had to test her. I had to see what she'd do on her own.

I ambled toward the stairs slowly, keeping an eye on them. Junior was incredibly loud for someone who wanted to have a quiet talk. "What are you doing with him? Your uncle called me," I heard. "You're being careless. You don't know what he's capable of." His voice was agitated.

A mocking sneer appeared on my face. He was afraid. I couldn't understand what Lily said, but she shook her head sideways and headed back in my direction. Junior played with my patience, grabbing her arm forcefully.

I immediately descended a few steps, ready to teach him a lesson. It wasn't like me to act carelessly. I plotted meticulous plans. That was how I built an empire. No one and nothing could get to me. Coldhearted with no feelings and nothing to lose, I was untouchable.

Thankfully for both of us, Lily had gotten away from him before I could reach him. She blocked the way, holding my stare with her shimmering golden eyes.

"I'm ready." She gripped my arm, then shot a last glance at this prick. "Have a great evening, Adonis."

Junior's mouth opened. I cracked my knuckles. He shut it. If a single sound was to evaporate from his mouth, it would be fatal to him. I ignored the flames of hell invading me and walked back through the stairs alongside Lily.

"I'm sorry," she murmured after some time.

"What did he want?" I knew the answer to that. *You.*

"Warned me to stay away from you."

I was surprised by her blunt honesty, but then again, we'd had a discussion about how much I hated liars.

"Adonis is a good guy—don't cause him trouble. He's just worried," she defended him.

When we reached the top floor, the valet bowed and opened the door leading to our private box to watch the spectacle. Between our two red seats on our balcony, champagne was served with aperitifs whose colors and flavors were meant to impress the guests with all kinds of caviar to golden cupcakes.

"Maybe he's right," I added. "Maybe you should stay away."

"I don't believe him." She locked her eyes with mine. "I don't believe you're like everyone says you are."

Lava flowed inside my core, trying to pass through the impenetrable iron gates of my missing heart. I ignored the jolt of red-hot heat licking through me, unbuttoning my jacket. Lily took her seat gracefully as I sat reluctantly next to her. My frustration erupted harder, knowing it was just the beginning of three long hours.

The light dimmed, and I swept the crowd with a glance. From the grandstands, their curiosity wasn't satiated. They peeked heavenward to us like a court watched its royal monarch. In another box further away, the Carmins were taking their places, and I secretly hoped I could crush all of them to dust at this precise moment. Melissa joined them, squinting her eyes in my direction.

If I were into dramatic gestures, I'd have rolled my eyes with annoyance. Maintaining a poker face, I focused my attention on my flower goddess. She was looking nowhere, sitting on the edge, her back straight as if resisting the sensation of collapsing in her seat. Her fingers rubbed nervously against each other.

I could sense the words of Carmin Jr. had gotten to her, but nevertheless, she was staying true to her hopeful self. Maybe she finally realized that trust was the most hurtful thing she could inflict on herself. It was a weapon you willingly offered. A destructive weakness. I wondered why she would offer me hers on a silver platter—I wasn't one to be trusted.

"I'm not," I finally replied. A knot tightened in my jaw under her stare creeping through me. My teeth clenched. "I'm worse."

"I—" she started before pressing her lips together, holding back her words. Soft golden lights licked the side of her face. "Isn't it weird, then, that... I don't want to stay away."

My pupils dilated, and my muscles went rigid as she exhaled the breath she was holding.

The lights switched off. *Orphée et Eurydice* was about to begin. The tense-sounding chords of the opera left room for the high head voice of the soprano as the violins raged. In the midst of all this tension, the ocean of lava boiling inside me screamed its own destructive opera.

I don't want to stay away.

Through the first act, that sentence resonated in my mind.

In the second act, "The Dance of the Furies" was a depiction of my thirsty demons.

In the third act, I couldn't focus nor find the beauty in this piece.

Orpheus gained the admiration of the world because he went to hell—easy enough. Yet, no one bothered to point out the fact that he was unsuccessful. He was foolish enough to lose his beloved. He wasn't a hero. He brought it upon himself while being offered a second chance. He was weak. Unworthy.

I peered over at Lily, curious to see if she was bored yet. She wasn't. She was magnetized. Her eyes glistened, her hands gripping firmly at the balcony railing. Her body was bent forward, immersed by the show. A carnival of lights danced on her face in the midst of the darkness. I couldn't look away.

Precious Lily, what are you doing to me?

I ground my jaw, the moment vaporing into thin air when, from behind her, I witnessed the stare of both Carmins stuck on her.

"Thank you for bringing me here." She beamed, not taking her sight from the opera, giving me the opportunity to scrutinize each of her features. "Don't you find this beautiful?"

Indeed.

"There is another way to watch the opera," I implied, her eyes drifting to me. "A double orgasm, I might say."

I'll be damned. My self-control was a vague memory, escaping me completely. The need to possess her was stronger than a hungry storm. Just like iron, I was indestructible apart from my own rust. Those undeniable thoughts she cursed me with were my rust. A weakness.

"Orgasm?" She gulped, flushing, whilst my stare traveled down the length of her whole body to linger between her legs.

"Only if you want to." A devilish grim line set on my lips.

She fell back in her seat, her heart leaping in her throat. She considered my offer, her doe eyes roaming my face. I felt like I was waiting for a death sentence. The judgment if I'd rejoin Elysium or the fields of punishment.

Her lips parted.

Her skin shivered.

Then, she nodded yes.

I ran my fingers down the naked, soft skin of her legs, admiring the goose bumps that spread. I reached to the slit of her dress, venturing closer to her groin. She gasped, her muscles tensing for an instant.

I inched forward, my lips so close to her nape that I smelled the sweetness of her scent with an edge of audaciousness and sensuality.

"We can stop anytime," I whispered like the snake corrupting Eve.

She gulped once more, parting her legs slightly in response.

"Watch the show, Lily," I ordered, my voice laced with my sinful infatuation for her.

She held her stare on the opera, her hammering heart enticing my darkest compulsions. I prodded at the hem of her panties, brushing the soft fabric. Fucking hell. She was wet. Hellishly wet. A bulge grew inside my pants as I fought the carnal need to fuck her in front of everyone.

She sucked in a deep breath when I teased her over top of the soaked fabric. I lightly grazed the crotch of her panties with my fingertips. Up and down, I let the pleasure rise in her slowly until she begged for more. Until she submitted to me.

Her pupils darkened, manifesting her flaming eyes. An amused smile curved on my lips as she tried to stay poker-faced when I ripped a part of her panties, pushing it to the side. I needed her bare for me. At my mercy. I stroked her folds and pressed my thumb down on her clit.

She drew her brows together, secretly holding on to the slithering pleasure. I rubbed her clit in circles. She met my movements, rolling her hips to my touch, trying to take control.

I wasn't hard. Worse—I was in agony. I swallowed my frustration, brushing her opening. I tugged her panties to create more friction. She pushed her hip forward, and I tugged it harder. A slight moan escaped her lips, and the thought of shutting her up with a kiss crossed my mind. Blood hissed to my dick as I thought of all the ways I could punish and take her.

She clung to the balcony railing when I slid a finger inside of her. I was roaring inside. I yearned to be rough. To abuse her senselessly like a caveman. To pound into her with the wildness of an animal.

But I didn't speed up the stroking. Not yet. I waited for the final moment to send her over the edge. I filled her up with slow and steady movements, her wetness pooling on my finger. She'd be the death of me. She battled to keep her eyes open, her nails digging into the railing. Her other hand clutched my leg. The strings and violins of the opera merged into a magnificent chaos.

I slid another finger inside of her. This time she couldn't contain her moan, loud enough for both Carmins to look over like hellions. Lily was mine. Her legs shook. I stroked her harder and faster this time, my thumb pressing and rubbing on her clit.

Her breasts lifted up in sharp, shuddering moves. Her eyes glimmered. A drop of sweat trickled down her forehead. I contained myself to not come watching her. I wanted to tear her dress apart. I was fury. Harder. Faster. Deeper. I stroked until her body quivered with ecstasy. She grabbed my wrist from under her dress before throwing her head backward to look heavenward.

"Rad—" she gasped but couldn't finish.

The moment Eurydice was sent back to hell, Lily's orgasm crashed around her like thunder. But I didn't stop yet. I let it consume her until the last second. Tears fell on her cheeks, and she held her grip tighter on the railing. Her eyes stayed stuck on the opera, and she bit her lower lip to hold the new tears that burgeoned her eyes. She was gorgeous.

She leaned closer to the railing when I pulled my hand from under her dress with only the desire to lick her. My heart wasn't steady; hers was about to combust. She found her breath while I gained a semblance of control back. I had no idea what had happened.

I was possessed. I'd gone beyond the limits, crossing an invisible line.

At this moment, I couldn't be more convinced that Orpheus was an idiot.

I would have done more than gone to hell for Lily.

I'd have haunted her even in death. Unleashed every fury. Conquered Tartarus.

I would have beaten the Devil and taken his throne.

I wouldn't have failed because I was hell.

We were a reverse Orpheus and Eurydice.

Lily was heaven-sent; I was hell-bound.

Applause rose as the lights switched on, and the final note of the opera illuminated the room of this tragedy. The crowd stood up from their seats, on their way to a night of gossiping inside the *rotonde des abonnés*. That was why I strongly disliked those types of events—the endless and boring talk of the aftershow.

I adjusted my tie, glancing briefly at Lily. "Let's go."

Her eyes widened with surprise, but she didn't contest. She followed after me, matching my rushed pace. I took a detour to *le grand foyer*—maybe as a reward. A large bronze and crystal chandelier, tapestries, vases, and paintings faced us inside a grand hallway. It was an ode to music.

Lily held me by the arm, intertwining ours in a knot that could not be untied. I kept walking, letting her admire the golden grandeur of it. We arrived at the deserted marble grand staircase. Alone, the atmosphere was more to my liking—austere, with flickering lights contributing to a game of mystery.

The doormen pulled open the entrance gate, and we stepped outside to the wintry night air. I regained my coolness, the infernal heat inside me dissipating. Lily folded her arms covered in goose bumps on her chest as I posed my hand behind her lower back, guiding us in the direction of the limo.

She broke the silence. "It was a beautiful night."

My driver slid open the door of the limo, and she entered, one step in. Her hair swayed with the wind when she whirled around to look at me. The blackness of her makeup was almost gone, the red of her lipstick vanished, and she was back to the Lily I knew. The one that did not belong with me.

I didn't join her, facing her like a block of iron that couldn't be melted. "My chauffeur will drive you safely to the manor. I'm not coming with you."

"Oh," she said, expecting more than I could give.

"I have business to do at the club." By that I meant do some serious supervising and occasionally conclude new deals. "I already spent more time than I should have. It's not in my habit to go out just for pleasure."

Each minute of my life was for the purpose of gain. Except tonight.

"So, there's something you can't afford." She chuckled. "Time." Her eyes dropped to the gravel. "Pleasure." Her eyes lifted again with an innocence I craved to take.

A ghost of a smile spread on my face. "The price to pay for immortality."

"Then I'm glad you offered me a part of your immortal time." Lily entered the limo completely. "Good night, Radcliff."

The door shut, and she was on her way to the manor. I strolled across the street, taking a cigar from inside my vest pocket. Lily was out of sight, but not out of mind—and that was something I was planning on resolving.

I searched for my lighter when my tarot set fell on the floor. I picked up all the cards but one. The remaining one flew in the air and landed on a puddle. I swallowed, hesitant to step forward.

The card called me from afar, having the name Lily written all over it.

This was the answer I'd feared since the moment I met her. Which card would Lily be? My instinct knew the answer to that all along.

I loomed closer. In the reflection of the water, the silhouette of a ravening crow appeared. As it flew above me, its harsh, grating sounds followed.

My eyes stopped on the card submerged by the puddle.

The answer was clear, delaying what was inevitable.

Loss. Destruction.

I needed to put a stop to it. I had to kill it before she destroyed me.

I was right—she'd be the end of me.

She was my number XVI.

Chapter 16

Lily

I was unable to sleep.

During the two-hour drive home, I felt empowered at the remembrance of being enfolded in Radcliff's dark aura. The night had been magical. He thought I hadn't noticed the growing lust in his eyes, but the way our flesh demanded salvation was impossible to ignore. I had never let any man touch me that way. I had never experienced that bolt of pleasure piercing through my core. And most unlikely, I was making him feel; he was awakening the dormant part of me. We were like opposite atoms balancing each other.

So, naturally, when I arrived at the manor, I traded my satin dress for my chemistry blouse and my sexual urges by the obsession of my mind. It kept me awake through the night, and at 2 a.m. precisely, petals became a precious oil. I had extracted the Devil's Corpse.

I rubbed my eyes and stretched my body on the chair of the lab. In the dead of the night, I peered through the window at the weeping woods, hearing the high-pitched cries of the huddled trees. The full moon was out, bathing their gruesome branches in a silver-blue light.

In this chaotic landscape, the greenhouse light constantly flickered on and off, as if a ghost was playing with the switch.

"What's all this?" I rose up from my seat and turned on the flashlight on my phone.

I exited the lab and arrived in the middle of the garden, my hair and my blouse swaying in the freezing air. And yet, I didn't feel the cold. A whisper pierced the howling wind, awakening all the spirits of the forest.

"*Lily… Come to me,*" the voice called out, like a siren causing shipwrecks.

The light of the greenhouse flickered on and off, gaining speed. I walked barefoot on the grass with the impossibility to detach my gaze from it. In each of my steps, I seemed to uproot the grass that clung to me as if to hold me back. I was so magnetized that I didn't dare to even blink, my eyes wide open on the one thing that had the power to erase the rest of the world at this instant.

"*Closer…*"

The Devil's Corpse was calling me.

My mind didn't have a mind of her own, obeying a stronger force commanding me to step closer. The light remained on, and a violent draught snapped the door of the greenhouse open. The moonlight illuminated the Devil's Corpse in a royal midnight-blue light. She occupied all the places in the greenhouse, the other flowers bowing to her in reverence.

I stretched my arm out in front of me, wanting to touch her.

"*Lily…*"

Thunderstorms groaned in the sky. The air filled with witchcraft and skeletons awakening from their graves.

The Devil's Corpse was alive, and she was monstrous. She displayed her vines—they were like the tentacles of a kraken wanting to grab hold of me. I froze, spellbound by the spectacle. The ravenous plant opened her trap and closed it to the rhythm of the angry sky. The draught was unstoppable, and it tore the door apart. The door flew away in the direction of the cliffs and from afar seemed to take the shape of a raven.

"*Let me show you,*" the plant demanded.

Under her enchantment and drugged by her smell, I inched closer and closer, ignoring the wrath of the weather around me. Her vines surrounded me like a rope and tightened around me. She lifted me, her petals grazing my skin softly as I arrived in her embrace.

"*Flowers take root in hell.*"

In an instant, images captured my mind in a flash.

Roots sunk into the earth.

Unstoppable, they opened the ground violently, forming rifts.

They continued until the pit of hell, where flames and skulls surrounded an empty throne.

"*You have to choose. It's time.*"

The Devil's Corpse opened her trap and engulfed me inside of her, her thorny teeth closing after me. She captured me, and I fell into the endless dark.

My heart leaped.

I jerked awake out of fear.

I darted my eyes at each corner of the lab. *It was all a nightmare.* I took off the piece of paper that was stuck on my face. *I can't believe I fell asleep.* I dropped my stare at the crimson-purple flask containing the Devil's Corpse. The flower's oil glowed with hints of dark green glitter. She looked like an obscure potion, straight out of a grimoire of forbidden spells and secrets of lost cities.

I let out a deep breath, and decided to fix the mess on my desk, wanting to not think further about my dream, which left me with a frozen chill behind my spine. My gaze fell on a word written in the middle of the paper, highlighted with two lines.

I must have written this before hallucinating. Rummaging through my research, I had discovered the secret of this flower. The Devil's Corpse held an insane number of pheromones. For the plants, she was attractive—that's why inside the greenhouse, she was surrounded by the wildness. To humans, she used her pheromones as a defense mechanism so they'd drift away by her repulsive odor.

I was convinced that mixed with the molecules of another scent, the plant would deliver me the key to the aphrodisiac—and of my perfume. It would allow me to transform the defensive pheromones into lustful ones.

A normal human nose couldn't possibly detect her pheromones, but mine could. Perhaps because plants spoke to me.

My excitement dissipated in a yawn. I checked the clock. It was 4 a.m. I finally made up my mind to go to sleep. Tomorrow, I had to be ready. A heavy day awaited me.

My nightmare said flowers take root in hell.

But their head was above the earth, looking heavenward to the bright sun.

And perhaps, they could grow one day to heaven.

Chapter 17

Radcliff

It's only four fucking a.m.

"I think…" Melissa interrupted my thoughts, her fingers brushing against my door before she sauntered inside my club office—uninvited. "I've never seen you drink."

That's because I don't.

I plunged my gaze inside the treacle color of my whisky, observing the bits of cork particles floating. I gave up everything that would have made me dependent, weakened, or influenced. I had total control of myself, until last night at the opera. I hoped the few drops of alcohol flowing through my veins would be enough to get rid of the memory of her and allow me to find my focus back. But it didn't.

I pushed the glass away from me and lifted up my stare to glare at Melissa from behind my desk. She sat on my sofa, displaying her crossed legs with a skirt way too short before pouring herself a drink.

"Go back to work." I had no desire to entertain any type of talk, or anyone for that matter.

"Don't be like that." She cackled, her manicured fingers sliding over the crystal glass. "I've seen you with her at the opera. She looked cute, but I have to admit, I don't think she's your style."

"And let me guess, you are." I pulled my lips into a sneer. We had been a one-time thing forever ago. It was short yet destructive and unpleasant enough to not want to do that ever again.

"You got to admit, Radcliff, you and I, we're the same. We fit." She shot me a dirty glance. "Neither you nor I are made for love. We're toxic individuals. Everything we touch, we destroy. I like sex and my freedom, and you are..." Her smile said it all. "Well, you."

She accepted her fate by swallowing her whole glass. She licked the drops of alcohol from her upper lip, her vicious eyes daring me to ravage her. Melissa was a player, but she was right. We were the same.

Selfish with no principles.

Taking our revenge on life.

Mastering chaos.

"There's no hope for redemption for people like us. We just have to stick together," she added, a glint of sadness flickering for the first time in her malicious expression.

I sank backward in my chair, my feet on my desk. I rolled my pen between my fingers, watching it spin like a wheel.

Lily. She didn't belong to my world. She couldn't match my darkness. She was born to shine. But here, she'd be the reason for my fall if I let her be more than a key to my goal. I couldn't let her intoxicate me. I needed to eclipse her from my mind, once and for all.

"That's why I found Christian," Melissa hinted.

If I wasn't so sinister, I would have laughed. Christian Carmin. The rapist.

Melissa was incapable of loving anyone but herself. She was either naive and stupid—flaws that were far from what she was—or she was plotting something with that maniac. After all, he was using her as a sex slave inside the private rooms of my club.

"Great choice." I couldn't be more sarcastic and uninterested.

"We're not official," she retorted.

When she rested her arms on each edge of the sofa, I knew it was a calculated act. Her top was open to showcase her abundant cleavage and red bra. She was smooth, but she chose the wrong battle.

"At least I'm not lying to myself with Miss Too Perfect for this World." Her voice was edged with amusement.

"You're jealous of her." Lily was perfection in its purity and simplicity. Melissa was just a temptation for the weaker souls.

"Please, she's a child. I bet she doesn't know how to pleasure a man."

I beg to differ.

And now the mental image of Lily's lips wrapped around my cock took possession of my mind. Stroking. Sucking. Licking. Her glimmering golden eyes would look up to me as I thrust inside her mouth. Fisting her hair. Guiding her to meet my drives. Deep and fast, to relieve my hunger. Slow and long, to watch her belong to me.

I snapped out of my illusion, aware of the bulge I had in my pants. My grip had tightened on my pen. I was no different from Melissa with Carmin. Lily was enslaving me in the most torturous way. I loosened my tie, gunning my eyes to Melissa. That should help me to cool down and become myself again.

My brows slanted inward, my irritation smoldering at the idea that Melissa could think this display of weakness was linked to her. I shifted the anger stirring within me to another topic. Melissa still owed me an explanation. I was clement with secrets; I wasn't with lies and people going behind my back.

"I know you're the one who locked Lily in my greenhouse on New Year's Eve." My hard, stony stare threatened her.

She gulped, her eyes widening in shock. I had eyes everywhere. The moment Lily told me about her fear of the dark, I'd looked at the surveillance cameras.

"Why did you do that to her?" *Tik. Tok.*

"I—" She searched for her words. "I just wanted to have fun. I was drunk, and I forgot about her on my way—"

"The truth, Melissa."

My icy, unyielding stare didn't bulge. Melissa was similar to a spoiled child. Temperamental, impatient, she broke easily. I was aware that in less than three seconds, she'd boil with anger, showing her true temper.

One. Two.

"You played the hunt with her!" she snapped. "You never play. She didn't deserve your attention. I just had to teach her a lesson. She thinks she's better than all of us, but she isn't!"

Inwardly, I was seething. Yet, I kept my anger in check, tempering it by swallowing the rest of the whisky. When I was done, the sound of my glass landing on the table thundered in the room. Melissa jumped out of fear and stumbled backward.

"Next time you hurt her." I rose up from my seat, my fists on my desk. "Touch her." I felt my face twist, my eyes reddening with an evil scowl on my face. "Or even speak to her, you'll pay the price. Am I understood?"

I turned my back to her, walking toward the glass window. I ran the pen nervously through my fingers, my gaze on the sinners inside my club.

"Yes, Radcliff. It won't happen again," she promised in a pleading voice. "I just don't get why everyone is after her. You, the Carmins—"

"The Carmins?" I spoke too fast.

"Yeah. Like father, like son," she snorted.

Like father, like son.

With a crisp grip, I broke the pen I was holding.

The pieces of it shattered on the floor. My father usurped himself into my brain. My nostrils flared. I felt my scar burning like lava waiting to erupt. The stained glass of my club sneered at my face. My reflection through the glass was just a mirror of the monstrosity of my father and his twisted persona.

What if I was just like him?

Nails grazed on my shoulder. "Radcliff..."

Don't touch me.

Like a beast on the hunt, I grabbed her wrist violently, smashing her against the glass window. Fury tore through me. I clutched her throat, my face twitching with disgust. I didn't want her. I was convinced that broken blood vessels were spreading like a virus inside my eye.

But Melissa smirked. She was enjoying this.

She liked my wickedness.

She liked that I was rough.

She wanted all the evilness inside of me.

She fed on my darkness.

She liked that I was just like *him*.

"Come back to me, Radcliff," she whispered, approaching with her lips, hoping I'd close the few inches between us. "Lily won't accept you for who you truly are."

She wasn't a quarter of who Lily was.

She was not even near a small percent of the desire Lily evoked in me.

She didn't deserve my wrath.

I pulled away from her, my heart pulsating in my throat. Seeing Melissa's arousal glimmering in her eyes, I knew what she deserved.

My indifference.

I exited my office, done with this shitshow. Now, I had to deal with two things on my mind.

One, the quintessence of good.

Two, the epitome of my own Tartarus.

Opposites, but both equally destructive.

Lily and my father.

Chapter 18

LILY

"**S**ometimes I feel like you have a soul, with feelings and stories to tell. That you understand me." I examined the Devil's Corpse closely, stroking one of her crimson petals. People said flowers don't have brains nor feelings. I never agreed. "Maybe because I don't have many friends."

I took a step back from her, waiting for a sign that my nightmare hadn't been an illusion. I got around the flower, but she didn't move.

"I must be crazy." I snorted and smiled at the thought that perhaps the only reason I connected with Radcliff was because we were both owned by madness.

Peeking through the greenhouse window, I saw Patrick Delange's car entering the gates of Ravencliff Manor. Impatient like a child on Christmas Day to receive the delivery of the oils, I shot a last glance at the flower. "He's here. I need to go."

She didn't respond.

I tied up my hair with the brooch Radcliff gave me and headed in the direction of the lab.

"Okay, Lily, you got this," I encouraged myself. After all, I was the witch in a cherry-blossom-colored blouse—because white was overrated.

The past encounter with Patrick was still on my mind, but it couldn't tarnish my joyful infatuation. I set up the lab and intertwined my fingers together, tapping my foot on the ground, eager to start. I counted the seconds, my heart beating fast.

A creepy feeling rolled down my back as Patrick arrived through the door. He was a totally different man, diffident and weak. His skin was as white as a ghost, like he already had one foot inside the grave. Dark circles had formed under his eyes, showing he hadn't slept for days.

"Good morning, Mr. Delange," I said, but he didn't move nor lift his eyes to meet my gaze.

His head bowed to the floor, and I felt like Medusa, whose glance would transform him to stone. His assistant dropped the batch of oils on the arranged space I'd made by the shelf before exiting the room immediately after.

"Are you okay?" I asked.

"This—this is your requested list and all the items you demanded," Patrick stammered, ignoring my question. He handed me a list with a trembling hand. "I should apologize, Miss Bellerose, for the way I treated you last time. I was rude and jealous. I hope you can forgive me."

I was puzzled. Patrick had one of the biggest egos in the perfumery world. Apologizing to an inexperienced, twenty-one-year-old woman clearly wasn't something he'd have done of his own free will.

"It's okay." I took the time to read the list carefully and checked on every oil. "Thank you. Everything is here."

"Per-perfect. Miss Bellerose, will you please tell Radcliff that I did as he asked?" With hunching shoulders, he glanced at me hesitantly, his thumb rubbing nervously against his palm.

Something was off. I felt the pulse of my heart in my throat, thinking of all the rumors about Radcliff.

"What do you mean?"

"That you're satisfied with the oils," he added hesitantly. A drop of sweat formed on his forehead that he wiped with the back of his hand. "Please. And if I can do anything for you, I'm here to accommodate you."

"No, thank you, I have everything I need but—" I approached Patrick, searching for his stare, but he backed away. "Are you sure you're okay? You seem tense. Is there something you'd like to—"

"Just tell Mr. Radcliff!" he bit out, his voice going shrill. At the realization of it, he rubbed his forehead, a mask of helplessness and fear forming on his face. "I'm sorry, I didn't mean—I should go."

"Wait!" I called after him, but he had already fled.

I fell on my chair, exhaling sharply.

Closing my eyes for an instant, I knew later today I'd have to confront Radcliff. I wasn't naive enough to believe there wasn't a dark part of him. After all, what type of man would ask to have an aphrodisiac made. I just hoped and believed from the bottom of my heart that I could reach out to his humanity.

But for now, I needed to focus on my perfume. After all, it was what mattered the most to me.

And for that, I had an aphrodisiac to make.

I need to go where no perfumers have ever been before, I promised myself.

The lab looked like an apothecary store. Hundreds of vials like potions. A full shelf of essential oils. Labels on hundreds of unsuccessful tries.

I thought the Devil's Corpse would have no mystery for me by now, and god was I wrong. Finding the chemical compounds of flowers was easy. Extraction too. But I needed to create a formula and find the right scents to match it. Basically, I was here to create magic—or do witchcraft.

Each flower was different.

Each flower smelled different.

The rules were that there were none, only beliefs waiting to be shaken and reinvented.

"I suck!" That was a cold fact, and I hated it.

I calmed my nerves and watched the sunset pouring through the windows. I decided it was time to call it a day—a failed, unavailing, inefficacious one. Simply, a waste of time. I threw my chemistry blouse on my desk, hearing the barks of Cerba from outside.

Radcliff. He was facing the cliffs with a sinister confidence. Hands in his pockets, his usual pitch-black suit swaying with the bawling of the wind. Even from the back, he was imposing in the midst of the unwelcoming forest.

I left the lab and stalked toward him, witnessing the fury of the crashing waves on the hard rocks. The violence of the scenery was an invitation to jump. A direct gate to hell. I remembered the urban legends telling the tragic fate of people ending their lives at the cliffs in hopes of entering the gates.

Even as I took place next to him, Radcliff remained aloof by my presence if it wasn't for the way he made his knuckles crack. He didn't bother to look at me, keeping his stare stuck on the ocean.

"I had my meeting with Patrick today," I said.

"I know." Still nothing. Not even a glimpse of the man I was on a date with at the opera. "Are you satisfied?"

"Yes, I got everything on my list, but I don't know, something was off with Patrick. He insisted for me to tell you that everything was okay... Did you—" I stopped myself from finishing the sentence. There was no right way to formulate the question.

"Did I do what?" He turned around menacingly.

He darted his eyes to mine and appeared soulless. His height made me feel like an insect he could squash. The depths of his eyes were a somber summoning to chaos. I understood my desire for him had been lethal. A cocktail of fear, agony, and chemistry, deadly to my soul.

"I don't know... It's as if you had threatened him somehow. He was afraid." And at this moment, so was I.

"I don't waste my time talking, Lily," he hissed. "Whatever I give, I can take it back anytime."

I ignored my hammering heart and my hair standing on end. "What does that mean?"

"It means I have the power to destroy anyone if I wish. And I don't offer reminders." His sinister tone froze my blood.

"You just want to be portrayed as a villain," I quipped back. "I don't believe you aren't capable of feeling anything. Everyone has a heart, Radcliff. Even the Devil."

By playing all those years the role of the monstrous Devil of Ravencliff Manor, he had lost the identity of who he was behind the mask.

He snorted like I was ridiculous. A blaze of fire burned inside of me, and a dull pain inside my heart was growing. I took my courage, inching closer to him, enough for our scents to collide. Floral met dark. Sweet met musky. I was ready to step in and nestle in his darkness.

"There is good in people if you bother to see the bright side of the world. I mean, love does—"

"Love," he articulated robotically, "is the biggest lie. It's a disillusionment of desire. A sin in disguise. A weakness."

"What happened to you, Radcliff?" I reached out to caress his scar with my fingertips. The muscles on his face tightened, but he didn't push me away. "How did you get that scar?"

"Stop what you're doing."

"Did someone do this to you?" I plunged my eyes to his. "At the church, you mentioned your father. Is that—"

He grabbed my wrist with a tight grip and pushed my hand away. "Lily."

"I need to know why you don't believe. I need to know who you truly are. I need to—" *Save you.*

"My father carved my fucking face. Is that what you wanted to hear, Lily?" he roared.

My heart shattered into pieces. The pulse in my neck thundered harder, and I stumbled backward. The sun slipped away to let the darkness take its place, Radcliff's face darkening to become one with it.

"I had no idea. I—" A single tear was forming, but I wouldn't let it fall. "Why would a father do that to his own son? It's cruel."

Radcliff leaned in, threatening and dangerous. "What if his son was a monster?"

His breath, so close to my neck, sent a frozen chill down my spine. It was like a plague, murdering each sign of life. The whisper of all unspecified evils released into the world.

I swallowed, bleeding the salt of my soul that poured from my eyes. "You're not."

His eyes glinted with something that terrorized me. "You're not ready for my tale, little witch."

"I am." Despite my trembling chin, I held up to his hellish stare.

161

"I'll give you everything you want in exchange to know what happened to you."

"I already own your soul, Lily."

A thunderclap hit the sky, and the dead leaves suddenly flew to collide with me. I clamped my fingers inside my flesh, holding in the hot torrents of tears begging to be unleashed.

"And your secret is owning you," I deadpanned. "You're afraid. You can't face the shadows of your past. It's haunting you more than you think, Radcliff."

A dark smile spread over his face. "Despite all my father's lame attempts at owning me, he never succeeded."

"Which attempts?"

Radcliff turned his back to me, shifting his head so his icy gaze with his grisly scar raked over me. "You want the horror, Lily?"

He walked away without a word toward the dark woods. A plethora of nocturnal ghosts welcomed him, and only a few seconds later, he disappeared into the gray, shadowed night. It was still one of his games. I had two choices—follow him and get my answer or stay in the blur.

I gulped at the air and let myself sweep into the dying nature. The moon shone in a silvery claw through a lattice of leaves as I smelled the rotting leaves and toasted marshmallow. I pushed aside overhanging limbs across the path, cracking the undergrowth with each step.

Radcliff stopped in the penumbra like he was born inside of it, cloaking the night royally. "Congratulations, Lily. You won the story."

I felt the woods were trapping me, narrowing behind me. They formed a gloomy cage with no way out. Radcliff was pitiless, making me face my nightmare to win his.

"He was the perfect rich churchman, a loving father and husband from the outside. On the inside, he made me his experiment. His guinea pig."

"W-What?" My voice edged.

The hooting cry of an owl echoed across the trees. My heart lurched, terror mounting in me with every step. Radcliff loomed closer as I bumped into an underbrush that tangled me, and twigs snagged at my hair. My hands were cold, and dread twisted in my gut.

"He believed I was possessed by a demon." Radcliff's words stuck in his jaw like inky venom spreading in his veins. "I was a normal boy, but everything I did was subject to punishment. He noted each of them in journals. Beating me wasn't enough, so in his insanity, he burned my fucking face, unable to stand the view of me anymore after my mother ended her life."

I was mute. A buzzing sound vibrated in my ears, as if a bomb had just landed next to me. My legs were wobbly, tingling, and goose bumps spreading.

"*That day*, I had made the mistake to believe in humanity for the last time." Anger rose inside Radcliff's eyes. "He played God and made me a monster. So, don't lecture me on human nature, Lily. You don't know a thing about life."

My body finally responded, racking with an onslaught of tears. Chills pierced me like needles. I was facing the cruelty Radcliff had suffered. His father had devoured his soul alive with all its wickedness, cutting and peeling him to destroy his own legacy.

"Radcliff, I—" *I'm sorry.*

That wasn't enough. Nothing I could say would give him back what he had lost. For the first time in my entire life, I was experiencing true fury. I wished I could make his father pay. I wish I could burn him the same way he burnt Radcliff.

"And here are the tears," Radcliff said with bitterness.

"I'm not crying out of pity." I wiped my eyes. "I'm angry."

His brows furrowed, and I snapped the dark thoughts out of my mind. I tamped down the pulsing anger thrumming through my veins. Pain couldn't fight pain. Water eased fire, not the opposite.

"You're beautiful," I murmured, my last tear tickling my cheek.

Radcliff's eyes drifted to me, and his pupils widened as if he had never heard that word before.

"You deserve better," I continued. "You can't make your father right by being the monster he wanted you to be—you're not him. *No one can take your soul away.*"

Once upon a time, someone had told me those exact same words.

It saved me.

"I don't have a soul left." He gritted his teeth. "Nor a heart. I don't feel. If you get closer, I'll destroy you."

Radcliff was towering on top of me. I craned my neck to stare into the purple calla lily of his eyes in a battle for power. The smoke of our breathing intertwined in a gloomy gray, while the heat of our lips was a few inches from meeting. Yet, no part of our bodies was touching.

I wouldn't let go of him after hearing the horror of his past. I was convinced I hadn't lost my sanity believing in Radcliff's redemption. Even if the price to pay was to be a prisoner, entrapped in my own body by my craving for him. He generated dark dreams inside my head. Most importantly, I couldn't head back.

I had fallen too hard to the abyss of my own hell.

Captured in the moment, I let the goose bumps conquer my skin. I let my lips dry. I let myself ache for the impossible.

"You're wrong. I know you feel it." I referred to the chemical attraction uniting us. That bond neither of us could have predicted. The impossibility. "You want me, Radcliff."

He didn't deny it. There was no point in it. His eyes, vibrant with arousal, and massive erection betrayed all the dark things he wanted to do to me.

Hurt me.

Trap me.

Sink me deeper.

The demon inside of me craved it.

All I wanted was one action for us to be set free. Sweet Lily wanted hell. Somber Radcliff had to show his humanity.

Without warning, he flushed our bodies together with a firm grip. He seized my waist with possession, trapping me with him. He crushed his lips to mine, owning me with ardor. Our kiss wasn't gentle; it was lustful. Savage. Wicked in the most delicious way.

My tongue met his in a devastating tornado, like swords dancing in an everlasting fight. He squeezed my thigh with his strong hand, and a moan escaped my lips. I was feverish when his nails raked down the skin of my legs until they reached my soaked panties.

I sucked on his lower lip like it was a drug I couldn't get enough of. I was unstoppable, gone with lust. He withdrew his hand from my panties to grab my neck, and stuck his other fingers through my hair to fist it. We instinctively melted into each other, not letting the oxygen pass through our bodies. Fierce and inexorable, he was a match to my determinedness.

Radcliff was my ever-bright flame.

I engaged back, giving him back twice his darkness by cupping his squared jaw, my fingers grazing the scar on his face. My whole body tingled, the smell of him heating me up to the point of volcanic eruption.

He engulfed me with his rugged arms, creating a halo around us, shielding me from the outside world so I would belong only to him. Protective and destructive. Safe and dangerous. Passionate and impenetrable. He was a contradiction, but so was I.

I craved more. I sucked and bit on his lower lip like an animal. I continued in my dementia a little too hard, to the point where I gave the Devil a bloody lip. But it didn't stop him. If anything, Radcliff's hunger for me was stronger than ever.

He sucked on my lower lip at his turn, claiming my mouth

without respite. My knees buckled, gave in, and he had to keep me steady with his grip. All I breathed was him. I didn't need oxygen. He invaded my senses, transcending me, and became my aphrodisiac. A delicious aroma.

I licked the blood that flowed from my bite. It tasted like an addictive fruit.

Pomegranate.

At the memory of my dream, I pulled away, out of breath. Our bodies separated, and my flushed face met his dark expression. What had happened to us? Blood dripped down from his lip that he wiped away with the back of his hand. We both gave in to sin. Together. For the first time.

"Radcliff—" I dropped, desperate and needy.

"To answer your assumption from earlier—you're delusional if you think I'd ever feel something for you."

"But you kissed me." He had kissed me with all the soul he pretended not to have.

"My point. I kissed you, trying to feel, but I didn't."

"Rad—" I sobbed through the tightening of my throat and a short intake of breath. "Don't leave me."

Our gazes connected, and for a moment, I believed he would stay.

But he didn't.

He left, stern and merciless.

I fell to the grass, crying my ripped heart out. I thought I would make the Devil feel. Truth was, he was the one who made *me* feel.

He flourished the darker side of me.

My Pandora's box had finally opened, and I wasn't ready to face my demons.

Chapter 19

Lily

The vial number 125 shattered on the floor, my dreams crashing with it.

It broke into tiny pieces, and so did my soul.

Happy birthday, Mom. I'm sure I've disappointed you from above.

My thumb was cut, my hand was shaking, and yet the physical pain couldn't match my emotional one. I would bleed. It didn't matter. I was a failure.

I glared upon the lab with disgust, feeling the average scents invading my nose. They were hellions reminding me of the moments I wished to forget. More than a hundred tries, and the notes weren't right. As for the base, it was soulless.

Instead of creating magic, I had created a pungent boring.

Failure. Failure. My demon was singing like a dark lullaby inside my head.

I had a brief. A narrative of seven words.

Pleasure.

Black.

Sins.

Heat.

Bliss.

Heaven.

Animal.

But the only narrative I had followed was: weakness, pain, heartbreak, fear, sorrow, hopelessness, and Radcliff.

In batch 57, my emotions reminded me that I was lonely, unloved, uncared for. I'd never mattered to anyone. The only way I could ever be was through my gift, but it had left me too.

Radcliff.

In batch 89, I had pushed myself to exhaustion. I came to the conclusion I had devoted my entire life to nothing. A numbness invaded my core.

Radcliff.

In batch 101, only the images of the way Radcliff had broken me remained in my head. The more I pushed him from my spirit, the more he consumed me.

I slumped into my chair, closing my eyes to hold in my tears. I couldn't fight back the pain coming in a wave, racking my body with chaos. My bottom lip quivered, and a tear fell on my cheek.

You're all alone, Lily. Always have been.

Radcliff not only spoke to my soul, he did to my demons too. He was the first person who saw through me, the first who made me feel like I belonged somewhere. I thought he could be the dark essence to my floral one, but he just crushed me and pushed me lower than the ground.

Tears spilled over the sides of my eyes like a waterfall. I'd failed my mother. I didn't have her talent.

The lily of the valley was a symbol of purity, sweetness, and chastity, but she forgot that it was also poisonous. Toxic. It was meant to be admired but never touched. A boring flower.

They wanted the ideal, but I was the spleen too.

All my destructive feelings came back. My fists on the table, I rose up, glaring with disgust at my vials. I squinted at the camera hidden behind the top of the shelf. *I know you are watching me.* A desire for revenge seized me as in a nightmare where you no longer control your body and your impulses.

In one brutal move, I swept all the materials from the table. They smashed on the floor in a requiem with high-pitched noises. The cracks spread, and the liquid, like blood, drowned the room.

The laboratory became a crime scene filled by black magic and destructive spells. Rage flowed through me in a corrosive liquid. I was hysterical. My heart pounded, and I picked up all of my research papers. I tossed them in the trash, wailing all my guts. I smashed and destroyed everything around me until the memories of my failure crumbled into dust.

Radcliff wanted me to be Dr. Frankenstein, but I was the monster.

Screw him, the aphrodisiac, the perfume, everything.

I escaped the lab like a fury, fully deciding to tell the fucking Devil that I quit, and would disappoint my uncle. After all, he didn't call me or anything. I was done running after everyone. I barged across the gardens with a destructive determination. I was in a mood for chaos.

My feet struck the ground in heavy clomps. Each step I took was as if I was destroying nature. I made each flower wither, uprooting the most innocent. I was in an eternal war with nothing to appease my molten anger.

On my way to devastation, I hadn't seen what was in front of me and hit Radcliff, who seemed to have arrived from nowhere. He was as strong as a spooky oak tree, rooting to the ground with all his power. I stumbled backward and lifted my head, the flaming wrath inside my eyes connecting with his shadowy stone ones.

Inwardly, I was seething. *Tell him off. Scream at him. Slap him.* I craved to hurt him, but I remained powerless.

"I know what you did to my lab," he articulated coldly.

"I'm not sorry." I wasn't. I felt a flash of irritation, and a fresh swell of bitterness rose in me. In a matter of seconds, I spoke back. "Actually, I wanted to run into you to tell you how much of an arseho—"

"You're cut," he interrupted me, staring at the dry blood on my thumb. "Are you hurt?"

"Why do you care? You don't bleed, right?" I shouted in a high-pitched voice. "Because to bleed you need a fucking heart! And like you said, you don't have any feelings!"

"Don't talk to me like that. Swearing is not pretty on you."

"And what are you gonna do about it?" I shrieked. "You can take everything from me—it doesn't matter anymore. I've nothing left! So screw you! Screw everything!"

Radcliff turned a cold eye on me, studying me with a critical squint. I couldn't stay in front of him anymore. I averted my gaze, a vortex of pain swirling inside of me. I stormed in the direction of the cliff, tears begging to spring to life. I was a mess—a temperamental, capricious mess.

"Lily!" he screamed after me, his voice hardening ruthlessly. *Go away.*

I ran. I ran to escape Radcliff. My feelings. My demons. The trees surrounding me were laughing at me through their scary faces. The forest was alive. But it wasn't magical anymore. It was a reflection of what was inside my soul. Horror and that wet grass smell.

I passed through a small tunnel, hidden by the rocks on top of the cliff. It led me to a hole. I stood at the edge and gazed down the cliff. One more step and I would plummet into the dark abyss of the forbidding stygian water.

I didn't bother to turn back to feel the chilliness of Radcliff's breath behind me and smell his dark fairy-tale and black-magic scent. He had caught up to me.

It was just us, in the middle of a chaotic scenery.

"Everyone leaves me," I whispered. "You know it's my mother's birthday today? Of course not. She died when I was seven. I was supposed to live with my uncle, but he didn't love me enough to keep me. He sent me to the sisters."

I turned around and swiveled my eyes toward him. Radcliff's aloof mask was decomposing with his eyebrows slanting inward and lips pressing together into a thin line. The veins in his neck stood out in livid ridges while he remained as silent as a gravestone.

"My mother was a genius. A talented perfumer. She was supposed to have the greatest career, but she had a dark side. She died from using illicit substances. That's why I swore all my life I'd never touch something destructive." I snorted. "That's how sweet Lily was born. I don't have her talent. Maybe I should just try to be like—"

"You're perfect."

"Perfect." I shook my head. I wasn't perfect—they all wanted me to be.

"Perfect to me." He ground out the words between clenched teeth.

That must have cost him a lot to say that.

"I don't believe you." I edged backward until the point my heel was halfway in the void.

The angry wind swayed through my hair, and I had to cling to the rock to not fall into the depths of the water.

"Lily. Come back here." His voice dripped with all the supremacy of a man who was not to be crossed.

Prove it to me, Radcliff.

"Oh, that's right—you're afraid of the cliff. It's cursed, right?" I concealed my pain with a playful smile. I wanted to push him the furthest I could. If Radcliff felt anything for me at all, he'd act upon it.

"Lily. I won't save you again. That's not something I can do. Come back here." He took a careful step toward me, spasms of irritation crossing his face.

Only one person truly saved me. My guardian angel. And he abandoned me too.

After all, I wasn't the princess type meant to be rescued.

I let out a wicked laugh. Perhaps I truly was the crazy witch. "I'm not asking you to save me, Radcliff. Go back to play the Devil, and find someone else to do your fucking aphrodisiac."

He cursed, his muscles stiffening. For the first time, Radcliff was hopeless.

"Lily, don't do this to me. Please. I won't save you," he repeated.

Rage gripped me once more. My heart raced like a trapped bird. "Why would you save me, Radcliff? It's not like you care about me—"

"Lily," he grunted, but I continued my dementia.

"I hate you, Radcliff! I wish I had never met you! I wish I'd never—"

I stumbled backward, losing my balance. It all happened so fast. The void invaded me. Radcliff shouted something in slow motion. My heart stopped beating through my descent to oblivion. I couldn't escape my fate.

One... Two... Th—

I hit the merciless ocean. The aqueous grave swallowed me whole, welcoming me to the Cimmerian darkness. It took me deeper, until I reached the aphotic zone with no hope to escape.

It made my lungs ache.

Blood pounded in my head.

My throat burned as if a sword had plunged into it.

I was stuck inside the river of Styx, at the crossroad of Elysium and Tartarus, wondering where I'd land. The air was being sucked out from my body. I didn't want to die here.

My body fought for every last bit of air, swimming toward the light. I emerged from the darkness, struggling to keep my head above water. But raging waves barreled toward me, attacking me. They crushed me again and again, throwing me back underneath the water. The salty ocean gushed down into my lungs, and I couldn't breathe.

The battle was lost.

Engulfed under the water, I used the last of my strength to peel my eyelids open.

I saw Radcliff's shadow through the light standing above the hole.

Before he disappeared, leaving me alone in the darkness.

Chapter 20

Radcliff

I told her I wouldn't jump.

I told her I wouldn't save her.

I gripped the rocks around the hole with force until the pebbles pierced my flesh. Drops of blood flowing like a dried-up river of lava were no match for the stirring pain inside my body.

The firm waves crashed against the shore like thunder in a storm. I couldn't watch her eyes frantically searching the area anymore. No one would rescue her on time. It'd be too late.

She'll drown.

There was no escape from the gates of hell that were swallowing everything whole. It demanded to be nourished.

A sacrifice.

I went rigid with a throbbing ache in my bones. That memory was too familiar. Pain ripped through my chest.

It hurt.

It tore me apart.

It was eating me alive.

My eyes glowed with savage fire at the memory of my mother's body crushing on the hard rocks. The blood melting with the ocean. Her ghostly eyes looking heavenward. The waves stealing her from her world. From me.

Make it stop.

I witnessed it all, and I was powerless. I was just a child, with a father that didn't care. Sorry, she said. Sorry, she haunted me with. Sorry, she cursed me in a loveless life. I had never swum again since that day. I never even dared to approach the water nor that hole.

Lily is going to die.

I clenched my teeth, no longer ignoring the agony I was facing. I felt. I fucking felt. All these crippling, weak, and somber emotions, they had a hold on me. I couldn't save her. It was suicidal.

Think, Radcliff.

Lily can't die.

She can't.

The low, gurgling croak of a raven snapped me from my paranoia. The creature faced me, flapping its wings furiously. It was staying put at the end of the hole. Its voice went shrill like an alarm call.

I thought it would attack me when its ghostly white eyes sharpened in my direction. A blind raven. It croaked again and again.

"What do you want?" I ascended into the same murderous falsetto of the creature.

The creature's eyes shifted direction, the waves reflecting in the reflection of its iris. But it disappeared the next second in the direction of the sky as if the message had been delivered.

I narrowed my eyes at the icy ocean. Lily's body was now underwater. She was gone. Fucking flower goddess. The cards never lied. She was my number XVI—the one causing me to fall from The

Tower. I said I'd go to hell for her. Truth was, I was going to Tartarus with no hope to escape.

It was a matter of seconds before I'd swim in the middle of the lost souls spinning endlessly in torment.

I cracked my knuckles and took a leap of faith at the price of signing over my immortality for a death sentence. I had a seventy percent chance of hitting the rocks, to be dashed against them. Twenty percent chance of being swept into the channel that went under the cliff to drown. Nine percent of dying of shock and having my brain get snatched. And one, of saving her.

I jumped like a demon banished from heaven. For a short while, I hovered in the air. Then, I hit the merciless ocean, absorbing the trauma of it with my hands. Pain lashed across my lower back, branching across it like lightning. Thrown under the dishwasher of the ocean, it felt like swords went through me, cutting me everywhere. The salty water hissed like needles inside the opening of my scars, wanting to take my flesh away.

Blood danced wickedly in the ocean as an offering, as if a sharp-toothed creature ate me from the inside. I ignored the crushing of my internal organs, searching desperately and savagely for Lily. After all, pain had been my only friend; I was used to it. Being pulled out by the powerful undertow, I fought against it. But there was no sign of her.

My eyes burnt from looking underwater for her, and I felt my vessels colored in a hellish color as they stung my eyes. My vision became blurry. I struggled to keep my eyelids open. The adrenaline took possession of me. I pushed my body to its limits. It was hell fighting hell.

Lily.

I perceived her silhouette from afar.

She was drowning further and further away from me. She was being taken away inside the abyss.

She would be in the shadows.

She was terrified of the dark.

I couldn't let the stygian water steal her from me.

I sank into my own aphotic zone. I reached out to grab her and held her body close to mine for us to swim back to the surface. The light was a tunnel that withdrew itself each second. I used all the strength of my sore body to pull her up, pushing her toward the light.

Her body was flying to the gleam, and for a moment, I thought of disappearing where I belonged, engulfed inside the belly of darkness. But she wasn't saved yet. I stirred the water in a wrestling match to reach the surface.

Out of breath, I emerged on the other side of the somber water, carrying Lily. I swam back to the shore, the current an ally. I was careful that her body remained on the surface. She couldn't die. I wouldn't allow it. I wouldn't fail like Orpheus did.

I fought the urge to peer at her. I swam as fast as I could, my gaze not leaving the sight of the bank. My feet touched the ground, and I carried her until we reached the beach. I posed Lily on her back in the dry sand.

The color had drained out of her face, her usually golden, sun-kissed skin as white as a ghost. Her lips had turned to a purple-blue. I checked her pulse. She wasn't breathing.

"Fuck, Lily! You asked me not to leave you, so don't fucking leave me!"

I placed the heel of my hand on the center of her chest at the nipple line. I roared at her between each chest compression. "Lily! Don't fucking die. I forbid you." I couldn't save my mother. *Don't die too.*

Again and again, like a madman, I continued. But nothing. I tilted her head back and lifted her chin. I pinched her nose before sealing her mouth with mine. I yearned for all the air inside my lungs to travel to her. I watched for her chest to rise, for any sign that I hadn't lost her.

"I'll hunt you even after death. You'll never escape me!" I'd continue my routine until the end of time if I had to. Thirty compressions. Two breaths.

"Radcliff!" I assumed Hugo had barged his way to the beach down the old stairs hidden in the rocks. Only a rope held them, so no tourists ever came to this beach. "Radcliff, what happened!"

Thirty compressions. Two breaths. I focused on my mission. My body created a barrier between her and the freezing wind; I was hoping to beat another element once more. Drops of my blood slipped on her angelic face, and I ignored the slamming ache inside my core.

"Radcliff, your face," Hugo gasped, throwing himself in the sand next to us.

"I don't fucking care!"

Again and again.

Thirty compressions. Two breaths.

Lily, come back to me.

My face twisted grotesquely. Hugo was calling for help on the phone, but I couldn't leave her fate in the hands of someone else. They'd be too late. The hope I had slowly vanished into the icy air. She wasn't moving despite all of my frenetic pushes, using all of my strength.

My view blurred, and I started reducing my speed. Perhaps we'd both die at the beach. My instincts led each of my movements, and miracle of miracles, her chest rose. I stopped, angst taking possession of me.

"Lily…" I sighed a low growl, my eyes boring into each of her features.

Lily's eyes opened slightly for a fraction of a second. A lightning bolt pierced through my core at the view of her amber eyes. She seemed to have awakened from a long sleep.

"You're back…" she muttered before her eyes shut again, and she fell unconscious.

"Hugo, take care of her." A vein popped out in my neck, my expression hardening. "If she asks, you rescued her."

"But, Radcliff, you—"

"Do as I ask!" I screamed, my gaze darting crimson flames of rage at him.

"You jumped… You jumped for her," Hugo realized, his pupils flaring under the shock of the impossibility. "You need help— you're bleeding. Your face is—"

"Go," I hissed.

He carried my Lily gently in his arms to take her further away from me. She would make it. My whole body hit the sand. I was drained of my strength. On my back, I struggled to hold my gaze on the rays of sun trying to pierce through the sky.

I heard the barks of Cerba getting closer—that careless dog was rushing to me. The beach was dangerous for her; she should be with that flower goddess and Hugo. My eyelids struggled to stay open. In the distance, I peered upon a bird darkening the sun, its shadow reflecting on my face. The raven.

Cerba arrived next to me, her barks becoming incessant. She snuggled into the hollow of my neck, her head on my shoulder. I felt her eyes gleaming at me with worry.

"I'm fine," I lied.

For the first time in a long time, I felt.

I was cold.

Weak.

And most importantly, I needed warmth.

"She's gonna be okay, Radcliff. She just needs rest, and so do you." Hugo tried to get some sense out of me.

I locked my eyes on Lily's sleeping face. She was tucked inside her bed, lights posed all around her bedroom in case she woke up during the night. I tucked a strand of her hair away from her face before drifting my gaze to the naked parts of her skin.

The fall had left bruises trying to—unsuccessfully—take away a glimpse of her beauty. She was miraculously alive—the worst could have happened. She could have ended up just like me. The thought of it repulsed me. I'd condemned her to the possibility of this fate.

But she'd heal.

The merciless ocean had spared her.

Perhaps, because her soul was too pure to be taken away.

"I'm looking out for her. You need to take care of yourself," Hugo insisted.

At my scorching gaze, he shifted, glancing at his feet. I loosened my brows that had bumped together in a scowl. I finally nodded, trusting Hugo with her. The searing pain of my flesh had grown with the lack of rest.

Without a word, I fled the room with long-legged strides to return to my own. I prowled the hallway, encountering Mrs. Walton walking back with fresh laundry inside her arms.

When she caught sight of my face, her eyes widened. She was slack-jawed, and a gasp escaped her muted mouth. The fresh towels dropped to the floor as she stood immobilized by terror. After all these years, I still disgusted her. I bent down to pick up the laundry and handed it to the old lady. She hesitantly took it, bowed her face down, and hastily left away from me.

Finally, inside the peace of my bedroom, I ran the water from the sink of my private bathroom. I took off my unbearable clothes that stuck to my damaged skin before peering over my reflection in front of my only mirror.

I was a beast.

The flesh wound was still oozing blood, my repulsive scar sewn up. Cuts were on my skin. I was stitched up like a Halloween monster performing in a circus. Everything about me was meant to be terrifying, from my imposing height, to the muscles I had developed over the years to be invulnerable, to my face carved by an all-devouring force.

My fists tightened on the edge of the sink. My bloodshot eyes manifested the wrath of the villain inside me. Rage flowed through me like lava. My lips twitched backward whilst my chin shook.

My fury sprang to life, and I slammed my fist against the mirror. It shattered, forming a spider's web with a trace of blood. The cuts of it distorted my reflection. My bruised knuckles and the pain were nothing against seeing my hideous self.

I was ridiculous.

I rescued her, but I wasn't the prince.

I was the monster.

Recognition dawned on my face—I needed Lily.

That was why it was time to let her go. She needed to get further away from me before we destroyed each other furthermore.

Because more than needing her, I needed those feelings to die.

Chapter 21

LILY

My eyes slowly fluttered open.

My vision was still blurry when I distinguished a vague shape in front of me. A halo of lights flew across the whole room, like dandelions that had been blown on. I thought I had gone to heaven. Each part of my body gradually bloomed. I felt like a flower whose petals had been folded during the somber night to awaken in the splendid spring.

"Lily, you awake?"

My vision sharpened, and I refocused upon the shadow. The forms became noticeable as my nostrils flared in the cold, salty air. Hugo was standing next to me, a smile dangling on the corner of his lips.

"That was one hell of a fall," he joked.

I readjusted myself on the bed, sitting straighter, my body

feeling sore. Blue bruises covered part of my exposed skin, as if I was a corpse brought back to life from her grave. Taking sight of my surroundings, I tried to place what had happened. I remembered falling, drowning, and then nothing. The oblivion. I searched across the room for Radcliff. He wasn't present, and my heart wrenched at the thought.

"I don't remember... How am I alive?" I couldn't tell what had changed, but my room at Ravencliff Manor looked so much brighter than it was before.

"I saved you. Saw you drowning from the beach and took you back to the shores." *The beach?*

"But what about Radcliff?" My brows snapped together, trying to make any sense of it.

"He stayed by your side, making sure you're okay. Now, he's gone. He went to work," he recited, all of those words ringing wrong in my head.

I held his stare forcefully, but Hugo didn't flinch. "How did you notice me from the beach when you rescued me?" I plastered an innocent beam on my face. "It was probably because of my screams. I'm glad you heard me."

"Right, thankfully," he moved on.

"You didn't rescue me." I crossed my arms around my chest and raised a brow at him. "I didn't scream, Hugo."

A squawk of laughter jerked his head back. "Well, fuck me. You got me like a debutante here."

My skin bristled as I took a shaky exhale. "He did it." Radcliff had saved me.

"He made me promise not to tell you." Hugo took a seat at the foot of my bed, abandoning his joyful mask to hit me with the seriousness of his face. "You know what the cliff represents to him, right?" I shook my head as a no before he continued, lying horizontally on my bed. "His mother committed suicide from that same cliff. He saw her dying."

Ashamed, my face went blank, and I brought my hand to my lips. The haunting tale of the woman who died at the cliff. All those times, it had been his mother. I had stupidly provoked him, tormented him, unaware of the pain he had suffered. Tears glimmered in my eyes. It must have been awful for him.

"It's my fault." I blinked away the tears, a tightening in my throat. Radcliff cared more than he had let on. He fought his demons for me. "I need to see him."

"I'm afraid that's not possible." Hugo scooped down and handed me a note on paper. "I'm sorry."

I wiped away my tears, eagerly opening the note.

You are free to go.

That was it.

I deserved only five words.

A fresh swell of irritation grew inside me.

"What does that mean?" I shook the note in front of Hugo.

"It means he's expecting you to leave the manor. Your debt is paid. You can go back to your life. He doesn't want you to work on the aphrodisiac anymore."

"But I—" I stopped halfway.

I had no desire to create his aphrodisiac. I didn't even know if it was even possible. But if it was, and he used it for destructive means, I couldn't live with myself—he'd break me. I had a chance to leave. But would I be truly free if I did?

Radcliff might have given me a golden cage, but it was a greenhouse whose door opened the kingdom of my dreams. With my uncle, it was a dusty cage with no hope to escape the boredom of my life.

I had to take a leap of faith.

Could I go back to a life without Radcliff? In such a short amount of time with him, I'd learned more about myself than in my entire life. He'd saved me in so many ways. I felt like I belonged. I was convinced from the bottom of my heart I'd be able to save him from the hidden scars he was carrying.

We were fated.

And most importantly, if I left, I would lose everything.

I couldn't let my perfume slip away. This was my only chance. I was so close to getting everything I'd ever wanted.

"I don't want to leave." I pierced Hugo's stare with dismayed eyes.

"Maybe you should. He's offering you a way out. That's not given to everyone." Hugo's voice was edged with malice. "He's a monster, after all."

"Maybe that's precisely the reason I should stay." *To let him see he isn't.* "I want him, Hugo."

"At what price?" he asked.

"The price of my soul."

He'd taken a leap for me; I was ready to do the same. I'd prove to him that love wasn't only an invented fairy-tale fable. I'd sacrificed my soul to make his aphrodisiac and my dream come true. The final choice would be his, just like it was mine right now.

"Radcliff will do everything to push you away at the price of destroying himself." Hugo's voice was laced with worry. "He spent all of his life learning how to not feel. You're a weakness he doesn't want. I think he needs something that clicks, a big awakening. An ultimatum in a way—which is what you've been torturing him with since the moment you met," he snorted.

A man was defined by his actions. Radcliff had created his reputation to hide his true self. The human one that I'd learned to get to know. I needed to fully accept myself to confront him. Radcliff was right about me. I was lying to myself until my deepest emotions caught me back, and my Pandora's box shattered on the floor, freeing small parts of my darkness.

I had to be his own Pandora's box—but this time, I'd liberate his heart.

"There is more to him that he lets us know. I can get to his heart." I swallowed. "You told me Radcliff saved lost souls. That he saved you. Can you tell me what happened?"

Hugo hesitated, drifting his gaze away from my pleading eyes.

"Please," I added.

"I was a troubled young man," he started with a smirk, shifting his body in front of me. "Got in many fights, used drugs, you get the picture. One day, Radcliff saw me waiting outside his club with a stupid knife. I was ready to kill some rich supreme white man who took everything from my family. He fired my old janitor dad after abusing my sister. I reported him to the police, but to the eyes of the world, I was just one more screwed-up nigger. No one believed me."

His mouth clamped, his face pinching with resentment. His tongue ran inside his mouth, as if he were trying to bite out the pain of old memories. My fingers stroked his arm, my heart thumping hard.

His past explained the blood I saw on his knuckles. We all dealt with pain in our own way—Hugo fought.

"Anyway, Radcliff prevented me from committing the biggest error of my life. He offered me a job as his COO after paying for my studies, and now I'm holding the shares of that bastard company,"

Hugo laughed. "Got that asshole fired two years ago, and he's currently on trial for rape with a judge he can't bribe—Mr. LeBon."

I smiled, seeing Hugo's face lit with victory. He obtained the revenge he sought. As for Radcliff, all this time he pretended to not have a heart. Yet, that gesture showed he was against injustice.

"I'm glad Radcliff found you. You deserve all the best, Hugo," I said, my emotions raising the hair on my skin.

"So do you, *doudou*."

"Can I ask you a favor?" I bit my lower lip, hoping Hugo wouldn't be reluctant to help me.

He shot me a glare, but I batted my eyelashes.

"Can you bring me to see him?"

"Nope, nope." He shook his head in a no, his gaze widening. "He's gonna kill me if I do, and I'm not kidding with the kill."

"If you want his happiness, you'll take me." I posed my hand on his and leaned forward. My eyes begged him like a cartoon character. "Please, Hugo."

"Christ, you truly are a witch, aren't you?"

I couldn't feel more ridiculous than when I arrived inside the sensual debauchery of Club 7 dressed in an azure empire-waist dress that made me look like a village girl and exposed my bruises.

I didn't fit the scenery. Men wore suits, women either elegant dresses or very revealing ones. All the guests' faces were hidden behind their masks looking like peacocks. *Great. Just great.* My heart galloped to the rhythm of the spotlights and neons, whose color changed from a reddish light to a dark purple one.

I scratched my arm several times, my eyes darting to each side of the club. Hugo had left me alone, being his usual social butterfly self.

I found my courage and crossed through the crowd, making myself as small as a mouse to Radcliff's office, ignoring the raking smell of sex inside the club. As I walked up the dark stairs, an arm blocked my way. I skidded to an abrupt halt. My eyes shifted to the side. Melissa had intercepted me.

I scrutinized her, a shiver behind my back. She wore a tight black leather dress that didn't hide her bondage lingerie underneath—probably not covering any of her intimate parts. A black collar on her neck. Latex glossy boots. It seemed to be some kind of fetish outfit.

"What are you doing here?" she asked, chewing the interior of her lip.

"I need to see Radcliff," I answered in the same bitter way as her question.

"He doesn't want to see you. Plus, he's in a meeting right now that'll keep him busy." She eyed my outfit from head to toe with a glare, crossing her arms on her chest. "You should head home, Lily."

"Please." I tried to reach out to the kindness inside of her. "With your help or not, I'm going to meet him."

"You should be lucky that I don't call security right now and throw you out. That said, I have an appointment inside the rooms that I don't want to miss." Melissa strolled sensually through the crowd, waving at a few customers.

I prowled after her. "Is Radcliff in one of those rooms? You have to let me get in there." I shrank inside the crowd, maintaining the pace. "I won't say you helped me."

"So, what? You want to go inside and perform?" She laughed sarcastically—the idea of me dancing was a total joke to her.

We battled our way through the masked people before passing an arch next to the scene, where curtains in the form of garlands acted as doors. It felt like we were entering a clairvoyant dwelling.

"I'll do anything."

"I see that, since you're following me around like my pet." She rolled her eyes.

We stood in a black hallway surrounded by red velvet paintings of body shapes. It had only two secret doors without handles. They opened through magnetic cards only. The area looked so secretive, as if what was hidden inside should never see the light of day.

"Melissa, please."

With two fingers, she held the magnetic card as one held a cigarette. "Radcliff will kill you and probably ruin your whole existence. It's the most stu—" She stopped, considering this with a malicious smile. "After all, I don't care, suit yourself. But if you bitch me out, I'll make you regret this."

I nodded when the door unlocked at the encounter of the card.

I exhaled shakily before skulking inside the room. I readjusted my dress, sinking inside the heated space. Illuminated by garnet-red LED lights, my gaze stumbled upon the wall of instruments facing me… Handcuffs. Harnesses. Some types of bondage elements. Rope. And something that looked like a big torture instrument.

The outfit Melissa was wearing made more sense to me. The rooms were dungeons. The scent of cigar and ashes masked every other scent. I swallowed, advancing carefully through the stage area with a fear growing in me and a bad feeling creeping down my spine. I clamped my fingers into my tender flesh, reassuring myself that all I needed to do was perform a three-minute dance.

"With your ownership as leader on the jewelry market, our partnership could fluctuate billions in revenue," one man added louder than the other men he was having a conversation with.

My attention focused on a chair situated in the middle of the stage. Curtains, like those for an aerial dance, were shaped like a swing hung from the ceiling. A mix of circus and cabaret in a red room. I gathered my courage, positioning myself in the center. I remembered watching the girls at The Institute for Young Ladies reproducing secret choreographies of stars—not that it could save me tonight.

"I don't gamble on probabilities. I want numbers. Your proposal is weak and my gains abysmal." Radcliff. The sound of his voice prickled at my senses.

I reeled around, peering at the shadowy shape of the four men facing me. They sat on the royal black couch and armchairs. They were so drawn to the conversation, I couldn't quite hear them. None of them had noticed my arrival yet.

One of them had enthroned himself with the force of an imposing god, his charisma echoing in the room. My pulse hammered—there was only one man who had this beguiling darkness. They all wore masks, but I'd recognize Radcliff's soul anywhere.

It was my window to push him to his own limit. I wasn't only pure Lily; he wasn't only the Devil. We joined in the midst of our darkness and light.

I cleared my throat, and the infernal light sent me into the limelight. All of them gazed at me, suddenly quiet. Radcliff ground his jaw as we held stares in a warfare contest.

The sensual music started playing, but I remained like a frozen doll. I had no desire to put on a show for those repugnant men, but the stakes were higher. *You do it for him. For you. For your perfume.*

"Is this a joke?" the man seated on the chair complained with an angry, sharp move of his hand. "Do something!"

The other on the opposite chair finished his drink and snorted. "We didn't order a schoolgirl, sweetheart."

I dug my nails deeper inside my fist.

I needed sweet Lily gone.

I needed to let the woman inside of me take control.

Do something. Anything.

"Is she gonna do something? Show us what's underneath your sweet virgin act," the annoying chatty one complained once more.

I held my gaze on Radcliff. Only he and the man seated next to him remained silent.

I distinguished a white satin handkerchief on the chair. I grazed it, noticing it had enough transparency to allow anyone to see shapes through it. *I'll show you what's underneath, asshole,* I thought as I pulled the blindfold to my eyes.

I shot a last glance at the Devil and disappeared behind the blindfold. He remained poker-faced, so I went forward and tied the handkerchief in a knot.

I grabbed the drapes of the hammock, taking a seat in the middle of the swing they formed. I felt my feet leaving the floor as I started elevating in the air. I tightened my grip on the ribbons, knowing that I was going to have to come out of my chrysalis.

I wasn't only sweet Lily.

A gasp escaped my mouth, and I let the thunder inside overtake me. I unbuttoned the top of my dress slowly, revealing the black lace lingerie underneath. The shadows of the men moved as they adjusted themselves in their seats.

Their gossip. The smoke rising. A lower lip bite to contain my nerves. All my sensations multiplied, a bolt of lightning penetrating my skin from an invisible force.

Despite the room smelling like ashes and death, I flipped my hair around in one sensual move. Dancing was the language of gods. If I had to dance on death, I would set myself on fire. I caressed myself from my neck to my collarbone, imaging Radcliff's hands all over me. Right now, it was just him and I; the others were outsiders.

I crossed my legs, securing one of my hands on the hammock, and I stroked the skin of my thigh, teasing them with the view of my panties. I imagined Radcliff's heart bursting with terror, his jaw knotting, his muscles stiffening. *Yes.* My other hand flailed above my head before I stretched one of my legs in an arabesque. I felt like an undead woman, each fiber of my body hurting.

Putting the pain away, I spun in circles, like a graceful tornado. My head looked heavenward, my hair falling on my back. Weak and devastating, I spun and spun. My feet curled inside the fabric of the curtain; I was imprisoned. My fingers tried to find salvation in each spin, to be saved. I turned again and again, finding the wildest of my own nature. The poisonous side of myself.

A black Lily.

I then held tight to each side of the hammock with a strong grip and let myself drift to the void. *Skyfall.* I moved my legs as if I was galloping on a field of invisible flowers. I was flying in the air, finding my freedom. The ground was beneath me, and I soared into the deadly air, in harmony with it.

I hit the floor in a half split. A ball of fire had sparked inside my chest, its grip transforming me into something else. I let go of the hammock and bent forward before standing up straight. I untightened the blindfold, letting it drop to the floor. The screen behind me had lightened up. It was some kind of inside of a futurist sex club—with red rooms and dark shadows of women dancing.

I reeled around with a smile. I'd let the madness and the trance have me. Demons would dance wickedly. The shoulder strap of my dress slipped, then the other. I strolled closer to them, meeting Radcliff's piercing eyes.

I wore my darkness with a cruel beauty meant to torture him so he'd come back to me.

Beautiful but terrible.

Our chemistry was undeniable; we had our own language. Our souls spoke in an endless torment and fought in silent war. The both of us were condemned to be sucked into a dark vortex.

Goose bumps scattered over my skin in colossal welts when I let my dress fall at my feet.

"Fuck, she played us well," the chatty man encouraged.

With a sudden burst of courage I hadn't known I'd possessed,

I swayed and twirled my hips like a belly dancer. I pulled my hair up sensually with my arms. My fingers danced to the sensual tempo of the music. *Radcliff*, my eyes called as I moved like an Egyptian snake. I hoped to be Cleopatra and Aphrodite tonight, inhabited by the same passion as them.

Radcliff gulped his whole drink with a predatory expression, watching me rub my body against the hammock. I caressed every inch of it with my fingertips, keeping my eyes locked on him. The intensity of our stare could have shattered the boundaries for this world to forge a new one.

I parted my legs, bent forward, and arched my back. My butt cheeks shook, each of my movements daring him to give up his control. I walked back like a catwalk model in the direction of the chair. I sat on it, my back facing them. I opened my legs on each side of the chair and grinned against it, flipping my hair.

Radcliff, I called in a silent moan, hoping to be the siren urging him to come to me.

Arching my back again, I let myself slip onto the floor from the chair. Lying on my back, I snapped my legs up together, rolling the part of my legs below my knees like a clock in a cabaret move. Not keeping my seductive eyes away from Radcliff, I opened my legs like scissors.

My belly then melted with the floor, giving the men a view of my side. I pulled my ass up and down, my hand trying to reach an invisible bedsheet. I slid to the floor up and down like I was making love.

Radcliff was close to breaking, judging by the way he eased his hand into a fist. The cracking of his neck. The bobbing of his throat. His lethal veins.

I pulled myself onto my knees, my hips gyrating. I rolled my belly and hips in a wave. Continuing with the floor tricks, I crawled on the parquet, my eyes flaming at Radcliff.

With a strong grip, his glass shattered and fell to the floor.

He had betrayed the fact he was boiling inside. I rose up, feeling victorious. I was ready to push him even more if I had to. But when I stepped to move toward Radcliff, one of the men had grabbed my wrist, forcing me to face him. His pungent, fishy smell invaded my nostrils, and I held my breath.

"Enough games, schoolgirl." In one move, the man shifted me against the wall with the objects. "Now it's time you let us play with you."

I gazed around in panic when the other chatty man took an instrument meant to restrain me. They and their disgusting odors wanted me at their mercy.

This wasn't a striptease; it was a wicked fantasy.

"I-I don't want to," I murmured pointlessly.

"I'm sure you like it, judging by the bruises on your body." The fishy-smell man laughed. "You like to be dominated, don't you?"

"No, there's been a mistake. I—" I was surrounded. I searched for any sign from Radcliff, but his stare had drifted away from me. Hands in his pockets, he wasn't acknowledging me. Radcliff was gone, possessed by the mask he entertained the world with.

The one who had remained silent approached me at his turn. His scent irritated my nose with something spicy. It burnt like needles or a searing fever. I grimaced. The smell was familiar to me. A memory tried to resurface, but the panic didn't allow me to focus.

"Let's not force a lady like cavemen," the spicy man finally spoke.

I thought he would release me. That I'd be safe. I was wrong. His fingers trailed up my legs to my belly and stopped at the curve of my breast. My hair stood on end, like a shield wanting to repel this unwanted touch.

"She'd be fun to break," he added.

I narrowed my eyes. "You can't do that."

"This one is a brat," the chatty one commented. "No one will make us stop. You stepped in voluntarily."

This was what happened in these rooms. Sexual games. Orgies. People came to hide their sexual tastes with masks from the face of the world. All these men were cowards.

I held my breath when the fingertips of the spicy man stroked the lace fabric of my bra to reach my nipple. My heart echoed in my ears. The foul smells made me uneasy and sent my head spinning. I snapped my eyes shut, hoping it was all a bad dream.

A draught passed.

A heavy sound clattered.

I was able to breathe.

I fluttered my eyes open again. Like a madman, Radcliff had grabbed the spicy man by his throat, slamming him against the wall. The feet of the man had left the ground as his hands scrabbled weakly at Radcliff's wrists. Blood dripped from the man's jaw that wasn't covered by his red mask. The other two stood backward, not daring to approach them.

Radcliff's mask had fallen.

He was hell.

A silent volcano that would devastate everything at eruption. Effortlessly, he had the strength of iron. Every vein in his body stood out. His mask fell on the floor, displaying his scary scar and hellish red eyes, flaming his opponent. Despite the snarl on his face, his calmness was even more terrifying. He was boiling from the inside, and something told me this was the strict minimum and nothing of Radcliff's wrath.

The spicy man shook nervously, the stronghold of Radcliff strangling him to suffocation. His feet begged for a release. I should have stopped this—that was the right thing to do. But I watched, mute, the life escaping from this man, breath by breath. My voice had been stolen, my right to speak revoked. It felt like a nightmare when you want to scream but it's impossible. Nothing comes out.

The room went cold as if all the lost souls of hell had joined Radcliff in his torture. Invisible shadows flew around him; they were at his command. Masks of fear were upon all of us, but Radcliff remained unmoved. Destructive.

"Get the fuck out of my club." Radcliff ground out the words between clenched teeth, throwing the spicy man away.

He crashed to the ground, coughing and catching his breath. He suffered Radcliff's humiliation, each part of his body probably burning and aching from the lack of blood.

His two other friends helped him up on his feet. As soon as he rose up, he pushed them away with a firm gesture before gesticulating furiously. He readjusted his suit and puffed up with self-importance, finding his composure.

He slowly turned his head toward Radcliff, clearing his throat. Radcliff's chest expanded as his shoulders pulled back. Fierce and dangerous, he was the king of that jungle.

"You made a mistake," the spicy man spat out.

The three men went off like cowards. The room filled with a heavy silence between the two of us. Radcliff's expression was tinged with menace, like a wild beast ready to attack. His breathing was sharp and heavy. He cracked his knuckles.

"Radcliff, I—"

With a vicious yank, it was my turn to crash against the wall, his violent grip on my wrist. Radcliff was pure anger, ruled by his demons. He towered on top of me, imprisoning me in his embrace.

His throat bobbed, and I hoped to counter the hardness of his face with the softness of my touch. I grazed my free hand across his cheek and scar, and nourished the hope to appease him. My dismayed eyes begged him to come back to me. I searched for his humanity, long lost in his expression.

"Radcliff, you're hurting me," I pleaded.

He loosened his grip, but fury was still running through his veins.

He looked away and cursed, "Fuccck!"

He slammed his palms so close to my face against the wall. Twice. I flinched, and my heart skipped a beat each time.

Trapped around his muscles, I was in his torment. He inched forward, gripping my jaw. I craned my neck to meet his stare, his sandalwood scent comforting me despite the terror of his eyes.

"You destroyed my reputation, Lily. You betrayed and insulted me."

"I know."

"You inserted yourself inside a business deal. You went against my order." His voice was thin and cruel.

"I know." I didn't apologize.

"You provoked me."

"Yes."

"I should have left you with them."

"But you didn't."

"You should have escaped me while you could," he prompted.

"You should have abandoned me while you could," I quipped back.

"I lost control for you. I always lose control for you."

I gulped. "I need you…"

"You're mine."

He crushed his lips on mine, hard and passionate. It felt like an electric shock. My senses were on hyperalert—I could see my blood pumping inside my core, my heart growing inside my chest, my skin bristling. We were plunging inside sweet chaos. I nestled under his darkness, tasting it with need, welcoming it inside my soul.

In a heartbeat, he made two handfuls of my butt and pinned me once more against the wall. His touch commanded both of my legs to wrap around his torso. I executed his silent order, molding my body to his hard one. He seized my thighs. I rubbed myself against the throb between his legs. Arousal descended down my stomach like butterflies.

I raked my hand through his sleek hair, which he captured to handcuff it on top of my head. He kissed me harder, and I surrendered to his strength, impossible to match.

Radcliff was the quintessence of power.

The epitome of danger.

The stealer of my heart.

I felt like the world was pale and grayish before he spun my world into a red-tinted heaven.

A formula that was his own, he enslaved me with.

The hellish fire of his eyes.

The pomegranate taste on his lips.

The aphrodisiac vanilla of his scent.

I sucked on his lip. The beating of my thumping heart slammed against his hand that had captured my throat. I was willingly at his mercy. Yet, I knew, from dusk till dawn, he had been my savior rescuing me from my invisible demons. His tenebrosity had slaughtered the ones hunting me.

He caressed, gripped, kissed my body with possession. He grabbed my breast with a need he never allowed himself to demonstrate. There was no denying, no coming back from this. We both took a side, fighting against the path we'd drawn for ourselves.

He resurrected me.

I bloomed.

I opened my petals, revealing myself freely. He was shattering each of my barriers to get to me with each of his demanding kisses. He replaced the deceitful lullabies inside my head with a song of his own. A sinful, delicious melody. When his tongue tangled with mine, the earth below me melted away. He exposed all the secret cravings that were dwelling inside my soul. I was soaking wet, a bolt of fire surging through me.

We sucked all the air in the room, stealing each other's from our lungs. We reluctantly parted away, and when I touched the ground again, my body went cold, missing the burning heat he had created. He analyzed me, animal lust brightening his eyes. A half-smile drew on his face, his soul demanding only to devour me.

He smoothed his tie before undoing the knot, leaving it hanging recklessly—which wasn't in his habit. He undressed his suit vest in one swift move. I took sight of his muscles almost breaking the fabric of his black dress shirt. Two buttons were disjointed—probably from the intensity of our exchanges.

He inched forward, wrapping his jacket around my shoulders to cover my half-naked body.

"We're leaving," he ordered with confidence.

"W-Where are—"

He swooped me on top of his shoulder, carrying me effortlessly. It wasn't romantic, no. It was a possessive gesture of a caveman. I was still exposed, his jacket not covering my butt cheeks. Cringing tight on his back, I felt so small, the floor seeming far away.

"You're mine now, little witch." His voice was threatening with no vestige of choice.

He wrenched the door open, and with long-legged strides, we passed through the hallway.

The last thing I saw before we escaped the debauchery of this club to start our own was Melissa's and Hugo's surprised stares.

Chapter 22

Lily

Time elapsed in a flash.

We spiraled inside of it, escaping its boundaries.

Trees. Gravel. The midnight glow. We probably passed all of them, but all I remembered was Radcliff's calloused hands skimming across my naked flesh and the sumptuous illusion of his lips branded on mine on the ride home.

It all disappeared into the air.

Moments were transformed into memories.

At our arrival at Ravencliff Manor, no one was asleep, and I couldn't stop laughing at the scenery in front of me. Mrs. Walton wore her ghostly white long nightgown, Mr. Walton dressed in shorts and socks going up to his shins. She had a shocking stare, while he displayed a disapproving one when Radcliff hurried me up the stairs.

Radcliff strolled past them at lightning speed as I gave a silly smile. In response, the flashlight that Mr. Walton was holding dropped and echoed through the stairs. Cerba barked joyfully, wagging her tail.

"Stay put," Radcliff ordered her with a click of his fingers.

She sat and whined. Radcliff wrenched the last door of the corridor open and disappeared inside. The air confined in the room whooshed out in a gust. The draught made my hair fly backward, as if a monster had just screamed in front of me. Stepping inside, it was like entering another universe.

And suddenly, time slowed down.

Radcliff's bedroom was a sanctuary for darkness. Despite the somber hues, the light persisted to enter through its rays. Curtains danced in the breeze on open windows, their fabric caressing the back of my shivering skin. Black satin sheets on the velvet bed were illuminated by heaven-spun stars. A misty gray sky colored by a glowing moon tinted the room in a wintry silver-blue dawn. The bedside light was lit like a melting candle losing its glow.

I gulped, meeting Radcliff's twilight eyes. He stood in front of me like a dangerous gladiator who fought the most Tartarian battles. He inched forward, and I lingered for his darkness to bury me inside his protective arms. I'd beg in deadly earnestness.

"There is no coming back from this, Lily," his voice whispered to my ear.

I don't want to go back.

A feverish wave of carnal lust swallowed me whole. His dark scent was like a plant emerging from the underground to take me into a starry sky without limit. A world in the stars, until the end of time.

I held my breath. In one swift move, my bra had fallen on the floor, and wetness pooled down my excuse for panties. I was wet. Soaking wet and embarrassed by the chemical reaction of my body. He had barely touched me, and I was already ready to collapse.

The intensity of his stare was enough to make my nipples peak hard at him. The dusky night our only witness, his thumb traced my lips before I parted them. After teasing my lower lip, his hand gripped my throat in dominance. The brittle obsidian of his eyes tested if I'd run away or if I trusted him. The pulse of my heart hammered on my neck, but I didn't back down.

If not, the desire for him to ravish me grew deeper. His calloused hand left my throat, and he descended his fingertips to my collarbone, my breasts lifting up at their approach. He brushed each of my breasts, tracing the curve of them with devotion in a ghost of a touch that sent goose bumps across my skin. Radcliff tormented my nerves, each second breaking my self-control.

He finally took a handful of my aching breast, and a gasp escaped my mouth. When he captured my nipple between his forefingers, rolling it and trailing circles around it, my eyes begged. Implored. Pleaded. I needed more. I furrowed my brows, rolls of pleasure electrifying my spine.

The broken god and the maiden. He had this instant supremacy over anyone. A sneer on his lips, Radcliff slid his fingers down. He passed through the butterflies heating my stomach to arrive at the strip of my panties. My hair stood on end in apprehension. Would Radcliff be sweet? Probably not. Would it hurt? Probably yes.

The thoughts of anxiety escaped my mind as he tore my panties apart, ripping them with a strong grip. The destroyed pieces fell to the floor. I was nude. Unprotected. Offered. Radcliff tormented me, scrutinizing every inch of my skin. But he didn't touch me. And god, did I want him to. He was letting me linger in agony.

"You're beautiful, Lily."

His fingers grazed my thigh, again and again.

Yes.

They always approached my sensitive area but never touched it. His back-and-forth on my inner thigh was a delicious torment.

Up. Up.

I was screaming silently until he skimmed his hand to my entrance. I bit my lower lip to hold on to my moan, contracting my belly when he felt my wetness with his finger. He teased my folds. I dug my nails inside my palm and squeezed my legs together, ashamed of the reaction of my body.

"Don't," he ordered, two of his fingers stroking my folds. "Don't be ashamed of your desire. I cannot wait to taste you."

Taste me? Another wave of burning heat surged through me. Radcliff positioned himself behind me, his fingers still on my entrance. Our bodies pressed together, his growing hardness on my back. At the contact of his lips on my nape, I threw my head back.

"Would you touch me the way you did?" I was out of breath. Needy. Desperate. I craved him to do again what he did to me at the opera. More than that, I needed it.

I could bet I heard him chortle, even if Radcliff laughing was an impossibility.

His lips pressed behind my ear. "I'll do more than that, little witch. Aren't you scared?"

I shook my head, lacking the capacity to speak another word. I pressed my pelvis closer to his hand, but he decided otherwise. He withdrew it, leaving me hanging. He massaged my breasts and tugged my nipples, continuing his luscious torture.

"I'm not sweet. Even in your wettest dreams, you couldn't imagine the dark things I crave to do to you. The way I want to possess you."

"I trust you," I panted.

"Bend over the bed."

"W-What?" I choked in my own breath.

"You heard me." The rasp of his voice couldn't be mistaken. It wasn't a demand. "Unless you want to back out of it?"

His words meant that he'd let me back away, but that was a lie.

His eyes captured mine, enthralled me with him as he tugged on my hair so that I'd plummet into his darkness.

I'd awakened his dormant beast, and now I was his prisoner.

"I won't."

Stuck between terror and lust, I positioned both of my hands on the satin sheets of the Victorian bed. I waited in angst for what would happen. I arched my back, my butt in the air and my face crimson red. I had no experience. Raised by the sisters, I was taught sex was a sin. It was disgraceful. Dirty. But the smell of it, of him, it was heaven-sent.

With his foot, he parted my legs, and my heart collapsed. A ripple of need ran down my spine, and I felt his breath beyond me. More shivers came. He trailed a delicious path, kissing the length of my spine.

He parted both of my butt cheeks before darting out his tongue. A cold, mouthwatering feeling throbbed in my entrance when I felt his tongue on me. *Heaven, yes.* He explored me in places only he had touched before. Pressing his mouth down my center, he kept my body in place by grabbing my hips. Sucking. Licking. Nibbling. Flick of tongue after flick of tongue, an unstoppable bolt of arousal grew wilder inside my stomach.

The pressure he put on my clit made me fall apart. My knees tingled. Buckled. I gripped the sheets below me as tight as I could. A tear formed in my eye. This was what it was. Desire. Lust. Losing control of your soul. I rubbed my ass to his face shamelessly, ground my crotch like an animal. Sweet Lily was gone—probably crumbling under her bed.

He slapped one of my butt cheeks, stroked one finger inside of me, and my mind went blank. *Fuck.* My face crashed on the sheet smelling of his addictive scent with a new note. *Patchouli.* I stared upon Radcliff behind me, devouring me. My mind was in mayhem. A burning mayhem.

He inserted a second finger inside of me, and I bit down on the sheet. It hurt. It goddamn hurt. I was tight. Too tight. I thought I'd scream. Cry. But then, the pain blurred the line with pleasure. Faster. Deeper. His tongue worked on my clit. Hot sparks appeared. My breath cut short.

Fuck. Fuck. Fuck. Bolt of fire. Stars. My orgasm snatched my whole being. I couldn't hold it—it swallowed me whole. Radcliff kept my legs in place, obligating me to remain under his sweet torture. I was shaking.

When he finally released me, he held my waist for a moment so I wouldn't crash on the bed, facedown. Instead, I gently collapsed on the bed, completely washed-out.

Lying on my back, I took sight of Radcliff hiding the shining moonlight with his masculine frame. He stood at the edge of the bed, still fully clothed. The curtains danced behind him, the cold breeze pushing him toward me. The room got smaller the more I kept my stare on him.

Radcliff advanced toward me, to claim me in a predatory way. I stopped him with the tip of my foot on his shoulder. *What am I doing?* As if my small body could hold him off. He, nevertheless, stopped.

I sat on my knees, pulling a strand of my hair away from my face. His eyes lingered on my breasts, his pupils dilating. I didn't hide myself; on the contrary, I felt empowered.

"I want to see you," I demanded, yearning for his strength to possess me. To see everything of him. "Please."

"I'll grant you only one request tonight, flower goddess. Choose wisely."

"This is what I want."

I felt my eyes glimmering when he unbuttoned his dress shirt. Each of his strong muscles contracted before he threw it on the floor, our gazes not drifting away from the other. Radcliff wasn't built like a man but an Olympian. An angel whose wings had been cut.

I flushed at the thought he'd reduce each man to weaken. None of them could hope to compete and compare. He was more powerful and threatening. The danger he exuded made me feel safe. He was a shield. Massive muscles like iron. Ripped abs with scars underneath. A fearless protector who'd stop at no cost.

He unbuckled his belt in a rough movement. His pants and underwear were next to follow. I gulped, noticing his well-endowed manhood. *Dear god, it'll never fit.* Then, he rolled his tie across his fist like a boxer before a fight.

I crawled to Radcliff. Standing on my knees, I lifted my head heavenward, gazing at him with a silent request to touch him. I took his silence as a yes and brushed my fingertips against his scars, from his biceps to his stomach. I hoped I would heal his imperceptible wounds.

Before I could brush his face, he stopped me halfway. One hand seized my jaw. The other pulled my hair into his fist. I had no choice but to bend my face further, my neck an offering. The shadows of his stare shimmered, and seconds passed.

He, finally, brought my face to his for us to collide. The way his lips touched mine expanded beyond the limit of my body; it sent me into a faraway galaxy. We swirled into a passionate tango. I bit him, he tightened his grip on me. I sucked on his lip, he possessed me with his tongue.

Mid-kiss, he entangled my waist around his forearm, lifting me up to push me further toward the headboard. I lay on my back as he unfolded the tie on his fist.

"Give me your hands."

I handed them to him, my tongue wetting my lips. I was in angst. He wrapped the tie around my wrists and cuffed them on the headboard. Entrapped, I boiled with need. Enslaved, when he kissed my nipples offered to him. Frustrated, when his tongue left only a reminiscence of a fresh, cold breeze on my nipples. That sensation contrasted with my body heating up like a volcano about to erupt.

"I want you," I dropped, hot and desperate.

"That's your second request."

"A request would be to ask you to end my torment now." *To make love to me.* "The second to be—" Gentle. Caring. Loving. The good girl in me screamed. None of those things were Radcliff. None of those things had made my stomach burn.

"I'd spare you of my need to take you roughly because I'm already taking your innocence away." *Don't spare me.* "But you'll enjoy it more if I do," he added with a mischievous smirk on his face.

I yearned for all of him.

The beauty and the ugly.

The twisted and the dark.

He towered over top of me, his sex brushing against my entrance. I wrapped a leg around his torso, counting inside my head. One... My heart lurched—I thought it'd break. Two... Radcliff seized one of my butt cheeks. Three... He squeezed it hard. Four... A moan escaped my lips. Fi—

Radcliff entered me. I gasped. My whole body tensed. My nails dug inside my palms. I thought he was fully seated, but looking down, he was far from it. I wouldn't manage it. I was a coward. A lustful coward, who had a pool of wetness between her legs. Pain and pleasure were like siblings, both tearing me apart to the extreme.

My skin quivered, my pain vanishing when I glanced up into Radcliff's eyes. One of his hands had grabbed the headboard, the veins of his arm visible from the tensing. He thrust inside me slowly. His jaw clenched away the darkest thoughts. He fought his urges and eradicated each of my barriers.

I parted my legs, pleasure winning over pain. He pulsed in and out, this time deeper and harder. He kept my hips in place. My chest rose up. My back arched more and more. I was openly naked to him. In each of his thrusts, he took a piece of my soul with him. The pain was just a vague memory. I was humming with lust. My body tingled, replying to him in symphony.

"Does it still hurt?" he asked between thrusts.

"N-No. It's—" *Fuck.* My eyes rolled back in my head as he hit me with a ferocious lunge. "You can do to me what you want. I—" *Dear god.* Another thrust made me gasp. "Show me."

Show me your soul.

"What I want?" His lips drew into a thin line, betraying he was enjoying this. "Are you sure you're ready for that?"

Another thrust sent me so close to hit the headboard. "Please," I panted.

The knot of the tie broke, and my hands were freed. In the blink of an eye, I was on all fours. Radcliff's hands ventured across my waist. Shivers spread, and he joined our bodies together. He slammed into me, igniting my world. His throbbing erection battled the butterflies in my stomach. *God.*

A salty tear dripped down my eye. Moans and gasps melted together. My breasts swayed. He filled me further, his hips pistoning me forward. I clenched my pelvis deeper to meet his forceful lunges.

He and I collided in a violent cataclysm. A sweet oblivion. My cheek grazed the fabric of the bed, strands of my wet hair on my face. The air I was breathing burned hot, and I fought my eyelids open to take sight of the depths in Radcliff's eyes.

Drops of sweat dripped down his strong torso as he mounted me. A line furrowed between his brows. It was primal. Animalistic. An exquisite agony.

"You can't escape me, Lily," he grunted.

My sultry dream came back to my mind. The red room. The heat of a sauna. Radcliff hit the end of me before slowing his pace. He captured both of my hands, handcuffing them with a strong grip and forcing me to arch my back. I felt him deeper as he lifted me up, my back colliding with his strong torso.

As he seized my throat with a proprietorial grip, the rasp of his voice whispered, "I'll go to hell to find you if I have to. I'll hunt you even in death. I'll tear each world apart. You're mine, do you understand?"

"Yes," I howled. I had liberated our darkest compulsions, plunging us into chaos.

I was his just as he was mine.

He released his hold on me, and the thunderstorm in the sky roared. His pace now hungry, his hands clamped on my hips. My legs shook. The room alternated between pitch-black and silver-blue as the thunder rumbled. He rubbed my throbbing clit with his fingers, making it clench.

We were both bloodred-eyed monsters.

My hips shot forward. He pinched one of my nipples and clapped on my butt cheeks. Again and again. I bit my lip until I drew blood out of myself. Until it hurt. Until I collapsed. Radcliff was without restraint, as merciless as the apocalyptic weather.

"Rad… R-Rad—"

I sucked in a breath, drops of sweat melting with a tear. All I needed was one last of his thrusts and my orgasm wrenched out of me in a fiery burst of pleasure melted into a sob-howl.

Radcliff followed in a growl. The thunderstorm stopped. The rain fell, and I collapsed on the bed.

The Devil's shadow on the wall.

A half-smile drew on my lips.

I had won his humanity.

Chapter 23

Radcliff

My breath was animalistic, heavy. It resounded above the tears of the gods. The rain manifested their sorrow to have stolen who belonged to them. The last drops of sweat dripped from my flesh; my primitive instincts were satiated.

"I'm sorry," Lily excused herself.

Her naked golden skin was displayed in front of me, contrasting with the cold, lapis lazuli night. She curved in on herself, using just a little space, yet she radiated the room. Her gaze dropped to the blood on the sheet. Just a small mark for so much meaning.

Lily was every type of beauty. Broken, when a tear tickled her cheek. Pure, when she covered her nakedness with the blanket—a blanket that I urged to tear apart. She was also a temptress, when her lips had moaned for me and her body responded with need.

She was a sumptuous destructive opposite.

I remained wordless, scrutinizing over her. The darkness of slumber had flickered inside her doe eyes. The red grips on her skin revealed I went beyond my self-control. That was just a tiny part of what I could do. All that time wrestling to get away from her enchantment had gotten me only more possessed. Lily was mine, and there was no coming back from it.

"It's just blood, Lily. It's nothing." It was everything. A sealed deal. Innocence for sin. "Come."

I held out my hand, which she seized. She rose up, and blood hissed inside my cock for a new erection. Her breasts swayed as she stepped out from the bed, and I yearned to kiss, possess, and take again.

Her skin shuddered. Her nipples hardened. Her pupils flared at the view of my cock hissing like a weapon. I fought the new wave of carnal desire slamming into me. We weren't ready for each other. She was too sore; I was too hard and wouldn't be able to exercise any self-control.

I erased the growing thoughts from her head that I'd take her again by swooping her inside my arms.

"Where are we going?"

I didn't bother to reply and carried her to my bathroom. I grabbed two towels from my dark cabinets on top of the smoky natural stone sink and dropped her inside my black marble shower. The metallic head that hung above us spread water onto our naked bodies.

The sudden shock made her flinch. It was cold. I didn't mind. But she did, merging our bodies together. Her breasts crushed my torso. Her hands and face hit my chest. I turned up the heat, enveloping an arm around her waist. I held her firmly, worried that she'd drop on the floor.

The water slowly warmed her, soothing the ache I created. I poured the soap inside my palms and massaged every inch of her goddess skin without exception—which didn't help to calm down my erection.

Her glossy eyes sparked to mine, fighting back a few tears. The way she looked upon me, with neediness, weakness, and blind trust was everything I loathed in mankind.

But then, the unimaginable happened. I felt my heartbeat. The dusty, grayish organ serving as my heart awoke from an eternal sleep, tinting itself in a bloodred color. It bled like an open wound. My body tensed, and I felt myself bursting into flames, as if a virus had entered and my molecules were fighting it.

The steam from the shower was thick, filling the air, and breathing was a hard task. It condensed on the glass, creating the illusion of a fog. The soap washed away, and I executed the next steps mechanically, ignoring that feeling of tightening in my chest.

I shut down the shower. I wiped the water flowing from her long hair. Wrapped her inside the towel. She obviously inhaled in the odor with a slight smile. I focused on Lily, drying her at the price of ignoring the drops of water running down my frame. I carried her again to my bed. Dropped her gently. Tugged her inside the blankets.

I sat down on the edge of the bed, watching upon her. I took my distance and let the silence fly, filling the room with unsaid thoughts. Lily's face remained flushed as she fought sleep. Her eyes glimmered under the moonlight, contemplating me with all her softness.

"Will you sleep with me?" she asked, her voice weak and edged with fear.

"Sleep."

Her eyes glistened. A lonely tear ran down her cheek. I stopped its trajectory with my thumb, making it disappear.

"Don't leave me," she whispered with all her sweetness, stroking her cheek on my thumb.

I'm not going anywhere.

I won't ever leave you.

You belong to me.

I cleared my throat. "Sleep, Lily."

The corners of her mouth turned up.

"You can't hide behind your words forever, Radcliff." She closed her eyelids, drifting asleep slowly. "Your actions showed me."

My lips turned into a thin line. She was reckless, convinced that having her as a weakness was a good thing for her. It wasn't. For none of us. I brushed a strand of her hair away from her face, leering over her chest rising up and down.

Lily was just like a diamond.

She allowed the light to enter and reflect off every facet of her. A diamond didn't reverberate in a rainbow color, contrary to what people thought. It allowed the darkness to penetrate and reflect in a silver tone. A powerful mix of darkness and light.

Too perfect, it'd be fake. A diamond had little breaks inside. Invisible to the naked eye, those inclusions were worthy to be seen only by a deserving soul. It didn't affect the beauty of it—on the contrary, it magnified it. It was those internal characteristics that created its uniqueness.

A bruised diamond, yes. But not too bruised to break and shatter. The duality I had for her was here. I'd hold the pieces together, shielding her, but my destructive craving for her could also easily damage her. Worshiping or enslaving her.

I strolled to the balcony, letting her dive into her dreams. I grabbed my tarot set on my way, observing the darkness with a new light. I shuffled the cards under the twilight. *The Tower* was behind us, but my gut told me this was just the beginning.

I was still keeping secrets from Lily. Things I couldn't tell her.

The prospect of losing her wasn't allowed.

The price for the truth was too big.

The only thing I was certain of was I'd protect her from everyone else—except me.

I turned over the card.

The hair on my skin hissed, and my blood froze. I let the card fall off the balcony. It sneered at me in its downfall.

A skeleton with an invincible armor.

A flag with petals of rose.

The boat of Charon floating down the underworld river.

The card no one can escape.

Number XIII.

The Death.

Chapter 24

Lily

Inspiration couldn't be tamed or tempered.

It was an orchestra swallowing me whole.

A symphony I had to play now, or it'd be lost forever.

My nostrils flared as I searched and frantically moved the hundreds of oils inside the lab. It was like looking for a needle in a haystack. The formula appeared to me in a diorama of images. The scents all collided inside my mind in a messy portfolio. It was just a matter of hours, maybe even minutes, before I found the perfect composition.

A pot of hibiscus scattered on the ground. It shattered into pieces, the soil dispersing. I glanced at the scenery, checking that the flower had been spared. Drifting my gaze, I took sight of Cerba, sitting near the damage inside her soft basket. I swore her eyes had narrowed, letting me know I had disturbed her peace.

"I'm sorry, cutie," I excused, rushing from one side to the other.

I was inside an unstoppable euphoria where nothing could hold me down. In one gesture, I slapped away the documents on my desk. They fell on the floor while Cerba crinkled her ears back. Even she knew how much her owner hated the mess, but I didn't care right now.

I readjusted my gloves, moving my fingers so that my hands would stop shaking. My hair stood on end, and my heart galloped at full speed. I had prepared the vials I would need, creating a mess in the lab. I was under the adrenaline, like a beast ready to emerge in its element.

"The answer I was looking for had been right in front of me all that time, Cerba."

I inhaled a shaky breath, my stare on Cerba. She rested her head on her paws, looking at me with wide eyes.

I then fluttered my eyelids closed and waited in a silent meditation.

I'd been drunk with scents since the sun rose this morning. Radcliff had probably woken up by now and read the note I left him by the bed. It contained only five words—just like the one he had left me.

Went to make perfume.
Lily.

On the *i*, I'd drawn a rose. Not that it mattered.

I waited for my breathing to calm down, listening to my heartbeat. I visualized the final piece of my perfume, my world gorging on smells. I refocused on myself and removed the barrier that prevented my emotions from breaking free.

I fluttered my eyelids open.

It's time.

I put the tube on my weighing machine, holding the pipette between my fingers carefully. The work was meticulous—a drop or more could change everything. By remaining concentrated, vial after vial, I mixed the oils with precision. *Pomegranate. Vanilla. Patchouli.* It was a potion, with all the scents that were connected to memories that had changed my life.

The aphrodisiac and the perfume were linked by the same formula—except that the perfume would follow the regulations and would not contain further than thirty percent oil. The aphrodisiac, on the contrary, was boundless.

Weighing after weighing.

Drops after drops.

Notes after notes.

Accords after accords.

The elixir of aroma was taking life.

But the secret of it remained in the base notes. The lily of the valley was my mother's favorite flower for a reason. It held a secret. It was the yin to the yang of the Devil's Corpse. Their chemicals matched in the same force. Darkness within light. The collision of both created the scent of...

Pure love.

Love was the answer.

I had been wrong all this time. My brief was so much more than darkness and sensuality. It was love. The powerful carnal passion it contained. The need and addiction it provided. The happiness electrifying your whole core and the delicious ecstasy it gifted.

Love was the most powerful force in the world, and now it'd be the most powerful perfume.

My whole body was boiling. Excitement melted in me as I inhaled the fragrance of the created formula. Euphoria wrapped me in an enchanting smell. I was close. So close. I was on the verge of creating a masterpiece.

I erased a drop of sweat on my forehead with my palm and restarted everything again to almost the exactitude of what I did. I was only missing the 0.001 percent that would make the sorcery of the potion happen.

One small drop for a perfume, one magic leap for perfumers.

Scents were linked to memories. I wasn't able to create love before, because I couldn't place the odors of it. I had to open my Pandora's box to face my feelings. To use them all. The good and the bad. The beautiful and the ugly.

The hell inside Radcliff had engulfed my demons.

The heavenly sky beneath my mother had twisted my life in a dark fairy tale.

I was now free to create the same illusion as the Devil did. A daily daydream.

A fantasy.

Breathless, I held up the crimson fragrance in front of my eyes. My gut promised it was the one. A burgundy smoke danced inside the vial, the particles hitting the end of it like fairy dust. I hadn't dosed it at the strongest yet. I had to know if it'd work first.

I grabbed a scent strip and plunged it inside the vial. I feared Radcliff and I would pay the price of our differences. Our worlds were never meant to cave in together. The underworld was never meant to rise above. As for the flowers, they flourished in the daylight.

I released the strip slowly. The aphrodisiac wasn't only the deadliest weapon. It was my key to Radcliff's soul. I decided to have faith in the good within the Devil. To believe. In a way, it was a hellish ultimatum. His redemption or my destruction. A gain and a loss. A balance.

A cloud of perfume filled my nostrils when I brought my nose to the strip. A bolt of heat warmed my belly, and my breath cut, inhaling the aroma.

I was transported to paradise.

Heaven.

Euphoria.

A tear of pleasure descended down my cheek.

The Witch had made the aphrodisiac.

Acknowledgments

To the young me who had the fictional characters of her mind for friends, the one who said she always wanted her life to be the one of a book, who was the weird, introverted kid living in her own fantasy world… you were right to never give up on your dreams. When you used to dress up in a princess gown before going to a martial arts class to show that a girl could be both the fairy-tale princess seeking romance and the badass heroine seeking her own destiny, you were right too.

This journey is full of ups and downs, of fears and passion, of overthinking and self-doubts, but in the end, it's magical. To all my readers, I could never thank you enough for giving me and my stories a chance.

I want to remind you that your uniqueness is your magic. I hope you'll bet on you and your dreams despite what other people may say or think. You're special and brave, and no matter which obstacles you may face, your heart and strength will conquer them all.

Thank you to my dear boyfriend, Lucas, who kept my sanity in check while I was writing this book. You listened to me talking (okay, obsessing) about my characters at every hour of the day and night. You're invested as much as I am—you're even making a fanart of them right now. Thank you for being weird with me and for showing me how to open my heart.

To my two brilliant friends I can always count on: Naemi, thank you for being here every step of the way. I'm so grateful we have been able to beta read and support each other's novels from the start. Blanca, thank you for loving Radcliff and giving me the best feedback and comments on the spicy scenes—lol.

And Mom, thank you for seeing the light in everything and for encouraging me to believe in my dreams.

Maria, thank you for your patience and for creating the exact vision of the cover I had in mind. To my editor, Sandra, thank you for your professionalism and for being hooked by the universe. Looking forward to working with you again.

The second book of *Scent* will be out later this year—and I'm beyond excited for what I have in store for Lily and Radcliff's story! You can follow my social media for the release date, teasers and sneak peeks, or if you want to chat! Each review, feedback, or message means the world to me.

I'm wishing you all the best,
Shanen

Printed in Great Britain
by Amazon

77885658R10132